CALYPSO'S ODYSSEY

CALYPSO'S ODYSSEY

ANNA ELLISON

HarperCollins Children's Books, a division of HarperCollins
Publishers, 195 Broadway, New York, NY 10007

HarperCollins Publishers, Macken House,
39/40 Mayor Street Upper, Dublin 1, D01 C9W8, Ireland

Avon a is an imprint of HarperCollins Publishers.

Library of Congress Control Number: 2026930076
ISBN 978-0-06-348504-4

Typography by Jenna Stempel-Lobell
26 27 28 29 30 LBC 5 4 3 2 1
First Edition

"I mean you no sort of harm,
and am only advising you to do exactly
what I should do myself in your place . . .
my heart is not made of iron,
and I am very sorry for you."

It's a lonely time ahead
I do not ask him to return
I let him go

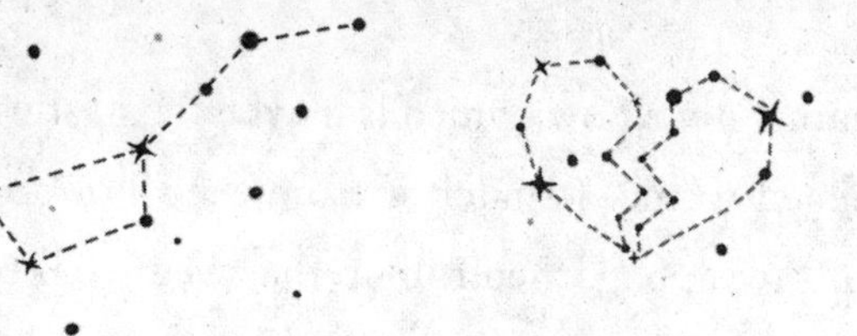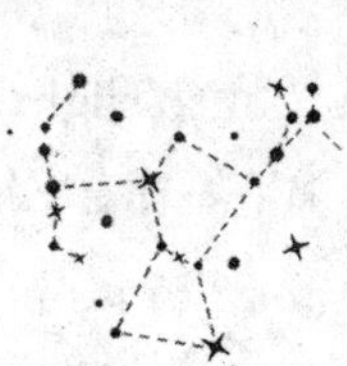

ONE

Another thong. Yuck.

Better than a used condom or vomit, I guess. Working at my family's inn, I've seen *a lot*—maybe not *everything*—and I'm really trying to bring a spirit of gratitude to this moment, to this day, that it wasn't something worse. I tiptoe around the pink lacy thing and go to the bathroom for a wad of toilet paper to pick it up. I'm already wearing latex gloves, but you can never have too many layers between you and a stranger's underwear, right?

Right.

"Ew, ew, gross . . ."

I don't know who I'm talking to—the hotel room's empty—but it needs to be said.

I reach down and pinch it between my fingers, which are wrapped in half an inch of toilet paper. The only problem is, the paper slips off, and then the thong falls and brushes ever so slightly against my elbow, which is maybe the nastiest thing that's happened to me. I snatch it from the floor and toss it into my giant trash bag, then roll up the sweat-soaked sheets and stuff them all into the laundry bin. Everything smells like sex.

I storm off to the lobby, only it's hard to storm anywhere when you're dragging a heavy cleaning cart filled with mini soaps and wet towels behind you. I'm halfway up the entrance ramp when Matty, the bellhop, takes pity on me.

"Let me help you," he says.

Matty's just old enough that he feels like an adult (twenty-eight? twenty-nine?) so I don't stop him when he grabs the front of the cart and makes it ten times lighter. We haul it the rest of the way together.

"I just got done cleaning room 18," I say.

"Hailey and Bieber?"

"Exactly."

We nicknamed the guests Hailey and Bieber because he was skinny, covered with ugly tattoos, and she'd definitely had some work done. The thing is, all the couples who come to Catalina Island do the same thing, in all the same ways, and when you've worked in the tourism industry long enough, you can anticipate their every move. Maybe we shouldn't dehumanize anyone with a nickname . . . but maybe they could be more original.

"Really repulsive," I say.

"Do I want to know?" Matty's hair falls into his eyes as he says it.

My dad has a rule that it can't be past his eyebrows, but Matty says he looks like he's in the marines when it gets too short, so they have this forever back-and-forth about it. My dad has threatened to fire him, but Matty's worked here for five years, and I think we all know that that's practically an eternity for anyone at the Ogygia Inn. Anyone but me.

"She left her thong," I whisper as we get closer to the lobby. A few guests take off on Ogygia Inn bicycles, headed for the beach. "It was practically in the middle of the floor too. Not, like, tangled in the sheets. What is wrong with people? The whole inn already heard them having sex last night. I can't believe they had the nerve to even check out this morning, just pretending that didn't happen."

"I got three calls, complaining," Matty agrees. "The older writing-retreat lady in 10 said she couldn't sleep with all the 'humping.'"

"Who says humping?"

"Her, apparently."

We take the cart through the service entrance, and I dump all the sheets and towels I collected into our industrial-sized washer, adding an extra heaping scoop of OxiClean, as if that might disinfect them. I know housekeeping is not for everyone, but out of all the things I could be doing for my shift, there's a solitude to this that I don't mind. You don't have to take drink orders or field complaints from wet towels.

"Should I just burn these?" I ask, only half joking. "I'm tempted."

"If that's our protocol, your dad's going to spend a fortune on sheets."

"Why does every couple think they're special?" I peel off the gloves and put them in the trash, then press the start button on the washer. "Night one—"

"Explore the town," Matty finishes my sentence. "*Do you know any cute restaurants around here? A neighborhood spot?*"

We abandon the cleaning cart in the washroom and head back toward the lobby. It's midday, and most of the guests are still at the beach, so the inn is quiet. My dad hates when we have any sort of side conversation within earshot of a paying customer. He says it's inappropriate and unprofessional. But for now, it seems safe.

"Night two—romantic dinner," I say. "And then banging. Lots of banging."

"I have set up too many candlelight dinners on the lower terrace. Do you know how hard it is to balance a food tray when you're walking down three flights of stairs?" Matty asks.

"I've only done it once. It is very hard."

I lean against the front entryway as Matty returns to his post. A grandmother is pushing an infant in a stroller around the lobby, shushing her, obviously trying to keep her asleep. The parents probably left them both for the day in a desperate attempt at alone time . . . or sanity.

"Then luxurious breakfast the next morning, and check out," I finish.

"And more banging," Matty whispers. "Don't forget the morning banging."

"But just . . . bring your underwear with you, am I right? Don't leave your room like a crime scene. Is that too much to ask?"

My dad steps out of the office, scribbling something on a notepad behind the front desk. Matty immediately swipes his bangs off his forehead, revealing a spray of acne. He stands up straighter and turns toward the road, waiting for guests who are not going to appear. Not only is the inn much slower these days, since our Tripadvisor rating dropped to 3.5 stars, but people rarely show up in the lunch window.

"It's not too much to ask," Matty replies, much more buttoned-up now. He barely even looks at me. "But I guess people sometimes do crazy things when they're in love. It doesn't always make sense."

There's a hint of sadness in his voice, though I wonder if I'm imagining it. Two years ago, in a swell of excitement, Matty proposed to his girlfriend. They'd only been dating five months at the time. She works on a dive boat on the other side of the island, mainly catering to wealthier clientele, and is extraordinarily hot. Like, could be a supermodel if she were taller (and didn't live on Catalina) hot. Technically she said yes, but now she's not sure, and they're taking space. It seems like they've been taking space for months.

My dad looks up at us, and I can tell that's it—Matty's not saying another word. I head behind the desk and check which rooms I still need to service before the end of my shift. I can feel my dad next to me, studying my face, and I try to ignore him.

I don't know when exactly it happened, maybe sometime after middle school, but we don't really talk anymore. Not about real stuff. When I got my first period, Pita, my best friend, was the one who went to Vons and got me pads. She taught me how to shave my legs and pits and bikini area and sometimes arms, because why not, and we went to the library together and read through one of those weird *You're a woman now!!* books. Even when things got really bad this year, I only told my father what had happened after Pita's mom brought it up to him first.

It's just different, having a single dad. I lost my mom when I was seven, and in some ways, I feel like I'm still losing. Dads try, but they just aren't the same.

"What were you two talking about? It looked very . . . lively," he finally says.

He organizes the last of the Ogygia Inn notepads that we give to special guests, counting them because there's no way he's splurging on more. Then he smiles at the grandmother as she rolls slowly past. I run my finger across the screen, then jot down the three rooms that checked out while I was cleaning. "Nothing, really . . ."

"Oh, come on," he says.

Am I really going to tell him?

"Just love," I say.

"Love . . ."

"And how people do idiotic things sometimes."

My dad's eyes are unfocused, though it looks like he's staring out the lobby windows. The inn is on the south side of the island, built into the hillside. The whole front wall overlooks the ocean and the narrow strip of rocky beach that lines the road. For a moment I wonder if he's thinking about my mom; he looks so tired and sad. Like the weight of the whole world is on his shoulders.

But then he just repeats what I said.

"*Love . . .*"

"Yeah," I say.

"Is this about that boy?" He turns to me, and I feel the heat run up my neck and spread out in my cheeks. It was stupid, thinking we could have an actual conversation. It's like he's always going from zero to sixty with the subject matter, and I'm expected to just race along, pretending we're besties covering all this ground. Instead it always winds up feeling too sudden and too intense—like a bad case of conversational whiplash.

"No, it isn't about *that boy*," I say. "Anyway . . . I have to go check on the laundry."

"Callie?" he calls after me. "Is it?"

He's all stern now, and I devolve into an annoyed kid, my voice turning high-pitched and whiny. "I told you it's not. Are you done now?"

I swear he says something about never being done with it, but I'm already pushing through the door to the laundry room. As soon as I'm inside I remember I put the laundry in all of five minutes ago. I busy myself with taking out the trash and organizing the mini soaps and shampoo bottles in the cart, all with our little OGYGIA INN logo on them. Then I sit against the wall, watching the towels and sheets spin behind the glass.

That boy.

AKA Harper Thorne.

We met in April, and he seemed cool. *Seemed* being the operative word. He was on spring break from his school in Los Angeles, just hanging with a group of friends on a scuba diving trip. He told me all this stuff about how he surfed, and how he wasn't sure if he was going to go to college. Looking back, it was like he was performing the kind of guy he thought I'd want to be with. Putting on this whole show. A week isn't really much time, and it wasn't until he was literally getting on the ferry back that his whole demeanor changed, and I realized maybe I'd been duped.

I told him I'd text him. Not in a desperate way—in a totally chill, we'll obviously keep in touch way. Because that was the next logical step, considering the fact that we'd hung out for a week straight and hooked up the night before. But then one of his friends kind of turned and laughed, just a tiny bit under his breath. *Sure*, Harper said. But it was like he couldn't get away from me fast enough.

The washing machine spins. Kicks up suds and water, the wet clothes thrashing against the glass. *Stupid*, I think. *How could I have been so stupid?*

I don't want to do it, but it's like my phone is possessed. Suddenly it's out of my shorts pocket and in my hands. Suddenly I'm unlocking it and pulling up Instagram. Harper and I were only connected there for a month, before he unfollowed me out of the blue, but I know his handle by heart. I type @Thorne988 into the search bar and his page comes up. His smug little face is staring back at me.

He posted just yesterday. He and a bunch of his idiot friends are on a beach in the Caribbean, the marble-blue ocean behind them. The location says Grace Bay Beach. I have to click to see that it's in Turks and Caicos, and I immediately feel dumb and uncultured for not knowing. He just graduated from Hawthorne Winfield last month, this fancy, billion-dollar-a-year private school in Brentwood that I also hadn't heard of until recently. It looks like this is their senior trip.

The post is a carousel, and in the first photo Harper is doing a handstand in the water. He and his friends, and some girls I don't recognize, are in another photo, digging a hole in the sand. He's squinting into the sun and smiling, and looks completely content. There are a bunch of icy beers at the edge of the frame. It all feels very light and fun . . . and expensive. Much more expensive than any vacation my dad could ever afford.

I put the phone away, but the visual lingers. That smug, contented smile. How could he seem so happy? Carefree? Like we'd never even met?

I hate to admit it, but it still hurts. It doesn't matter how much I want to be over it. Matty was right—people do stupid things for love.

I just never thought one of those stupid people would be me.

TWO

FOUR DAYS BEFORE ODIE

As soon as my shift ends, I'm out of there, cutting down the stairs that hug the side of the inn. The four-story, beachy, shingled building was built into the hillside in the seventies, and I pass almost every room as I zigzag down its side. Above me, the wind chimes clink in the breeze. When I get to the road I brush my hand against the shell mosaic, the way I always do, just to steady myself. When I was little, my mom decorated the inn's five-foot foundation with hundreds of polished abalone shells. The effect is a swirling, iridescent artwork that is different colors depending on the time of day.

I must've taken those steps a thousand times. Up and down in my mother's arms, then, once she got sick, my father's. It's a short walk down Pebbly Beach Road to the beach, but as soon as I get there, I take off my sneakers and let my feet grip the rocks. I try to visit every morning and every night, just to feel the wind kick up off the ocean. The rocks are grounding—the sound of them clanking together as I walk, the slight adjustment my body makes every time they shift under my feet. No matter how bad things get, or how lost I feel, just ten minutes here is enough to return me to myself. To feel human again.

Tonight the sun is still warm on the horizon, casting an orange glow. I turn back, taking in the inn behind me. The gray paint is buckled and peeling, and there are several shingles missing. It's still stunning—it's the only building on this part of the island, and it basically looks like it's carved into the rock. But then my eyes settle on the windows of room 2. The curtains have been permanently drawn for months now. If I'm being honest, that feels like where all our bad luck started. It's the only room on the bottom floor of the inn, so it wasn't obvious when the water damage started. A guest reported it to us, then to Yelp, with a scathing review. Every time my dad thought he'd fixed it, another leak would spring somewhere else, and another guest would be furious, and suddenly we had this reputation for being a dingy budget hotel, somewhere you'd only stay if all the other places in Avalon were booked up.

Last year he finally decided to just close the room entirely, after Kai, our family friend who runs one of the only construction companies on the island, priced out what it would take to really get it fixed. It needed everything from new drywall to its own separate plumbing, and my dad was like, *To hell with it. It isn't worth it.* But now we have this decrepit room that you can see every time you come up from the beach. It's giving haunted house vibes.

If we weren't a budget inn before, we definitely are now.

As I get farther away from the inn, the beach widens. The old hippies are here today, parked in their usual spot, doors open, their Fiat blasting New Age music from the speakers. Pita and I have been coming here for the past couple years, basically as soon as we were allowed to hang at the beach alone. I can see her all the way at the end, spread out on a striped blanket, her eyes closed against the setting sun.

"Incoming!" I yell as soon as I'm close enough. Then I dive onto the blanket beside her, nuzzling my face into her warm bare shoulder. She smells of sunblock and salty ocean water. Her hair is stringy from being out here all day.

"My favorite beach bomber," she says without opening her eyes. "How was work?"

"Eh."

"I took the liberty of picking up dinner."

Then she finally turns over and pulls a massive sub from her tote. ISLAND EATERY is printed all over the parchment paper. Pita's been working there three days a week since our junior year, but Tuesday is always her day off.

"What am I going to do when I have to pay for my sandwiches?" I ask.

"Please. Bo is obsessed with you. I'm pretty sure you're getting free sandwiches for life."

"Bo is fourteen. Gross."

"He likes older women." Pita shrugs. "What can I say?"

There's something endlessly depressing about thinking of Pita away at UC Santa Cruz next year and me still here, on Catalina, going into Island Eatery when she's not there. Shooting the shit with Bo, hoping he'll give me a free sandwich. He doesn't even shave yet and has one of those skeevy wispy mustaches.

Yes, their Italian subs are incredible, and it's basically the only place you can get them on Catalina, but no. Just no.

Pita puts on her sunglasses and unwraps the sandwich the same way she wraps them—with fast, expert hands that unfold the thin foil underneath so it all stays intact. She passes me half and we take our first bites in silence, staring out at the ocean.

There are only ever locals at this beach. If pressed, I could probably tell you every single person's name (or at least their first name). The guys in the water are a year behind us in school, led by Ziggy, this sweet junior who all the freshmen are obsessed with. Yesenia and Kate, two girls Pita and I like but don't hang out with, are at the water's edge, up to their ankles. A retired couple who live up on Oak Road are in their usual folding lounge chairs. They've been cooking out here all day, their skin as brown and crisp as a roast turkey's.

I take down another bite. The mayo and mustard are all swirled together, mixing with some pepperoncini to create the perfect spread. "Fuck yes. This sandwich . . ."

"Orgasmic," Pita says.

"Yes, *mmmmm!*" I moan, then take another bite. "They

don't have anything like this in Santa Cruz. I bet it's all vegan chips and gluten-free bread."

It sounds a little bitter, the way it comes out, which I didn't expect. I laugh awkwardly, trying to pretend it was just a joke, but Pita is already leaning against me, putting her full weight on my shoulder. I have to literally push back to keep from falling over.

"You know I'm going to miss you so much it's stupid," she says.

"That doesn't make me feel any better."

"You can come visit."

"All your new college friends are going to be like: *So, what school do you go to?* And I'm going to have to be like: *Oh, I don't go to college. I just work at my family's hotel. Cleaning the sheets and dealing with annoying guests who keep asking why we don't have Wi-Fi.*"

"Or you could just lie, like a normal person. Say you're taking a gap year."

"Right. Also an option."

Pita swallows another bite.

"People take gap years. It sounds really fancy."

It doesn't feel fancy. Not at all. I wasn't sure where I wanted to apply, then I couldn't get my applications together in time, and even the schools I could get into weren't ones I actually wanted to go to. Now it feels like maybe one year will stretch into five, and then ten, and I'll wake up and still be working at my dad's inn, still be vacuuming rooms and throwing out someone else's crusty thong. My plan was to reapply next year, or maybe even apply to culinary school—something I've always wanted to do but am kind of nervous about. Of all the jobs I've had at the inn, my favorite has always been sous cheffing in the kitchen. At one point I was doing most of the prep work too, but after everything happened my dad thought it might be better if I scale back my hours.

"Or you could say you're working at your family business. That you're thinking of taking it over," she says.

"I'm not, though."

"But it sounds important. And entrepreneurial."

"Ahhh, good idea," I lie, pretending I'll take her advice.

"You'll come visit," she repeats. "You'll be there so much it'll be like you're going to UC Santa Cruz too. My friends will be your friends."

"I know," I say. But that's lie number two. I don't know if Pita is being delusional or what, but I've mapped it every way possible. UC Santa Cruz is right below San Francisco. To even visit, I'd have to take the ferry to Long Beach, then rent a car and drive up the coast for over six hours. It would be at least an eight-hour journey each way. I guess I could fly, but it's not like flights are cheap.

Pita adjusts the straps of her string bikini top, untying and tying them again. She's crazy beautiful, with perfect, perky boobs and long black hair that goes halfway down her back. Her brown eyes have the kind of thick black lashes you see on babies.

"Also, it's only a year," Pita says. "Who knows where you'll be after that."

"I'll probably still be here."

"No you won't. You have a year to do anything. You could intern at the medical center, or start working on one of the dive boats. You just have to find something interesting to write about for your essays. Something that stands out. You have until next year to get your applications together."

"I don't want to intern at the medical center," I say. "I deal with enough tourists already."

"It could be anything."

"Right."

What I really want to say is that I'd need a scholarship for school, since the finances of the inn, which are *our* finances, are . . . not good. I don't know how "not good" they are; I just know that more and more envelopes show up with things like PAST DUE and LAST NOTICE written on them, and every time I try to ask my dad he says not to worry, that everything's fine. But things definitely don't seem fine.

"I might take a swim," I say.

"Oh . . . cool. I'll be here."

I peel off my T-shirt and shorts, shimmying down to the cherry-red bikini underneath. It's not a Speedo, but the top is basically a cropped tank, tight enough I can really swim and not have to worry. I sink into the water without looking back.

Four steps and I'm in, diving beneath the surface. I've always been a strong swimmer, but after my mom got sick it was my way of coping. Underwater, no one was talking about chemotherapy and hospice and morphine doses. In the ocean I felt strong, powerful.

I swim out until Pita is just a little speck on the sand, until I can barely hear the guys chatting, their wet suits glistening like seals in the sun. I rip across the ocean, where the water is deeper. It is clear and still and so blue, like something out of a movie. I go back and forth, swimming laps until I tire myself out. When I can't swim anymore I float for a while, letting the last of the sun warm my cheeks. It feels like forever has passed when my feet finally get back on land. My knees are unsteady from so much time in the sea.

A small group of boys I don't recognize has crowded around Pita. They're tourists—it's always obvious. They're much paler than us locals, and their bathing suits and backpacks are all designer brands. I can spot their Tom Ford flip-flops a mile away. I cross my arms over my chest as I walk toward them, grabbing my towel as soon as possible and wrapping it around my torso.

"Hey." One of the boys nods at me. He's tall and ropy, with light blue eyes.

"These guys are visiting for the weekend," Pita says.

"How'd you hear about this beach?" I ask.

It sounds a little pointed, because it is. It's not on any maps. Most tourists zip right past on their golf cart tours, barely even noticing it.

"Reddit," a short kid with dreadlocks says.

"I do everything Reddit says," the blue-eyed kid says.

"Well, that's a red flag if I've ever heard one," I say.

The third boy, who's standing behind the other two, laughs. "We didn't even catch your names . . ." He has a blue terry cloth towel around his shoulders, and shaggy black hair that's kind of poufy in the front. He looks from me to Pita.

"Pita," she says. "And this is Callie."

I wait for them to do what most dumbasses do . . . *Pita, like the chip?* Pita's full name is Lupita—her parents are Mexican American—but she's always gone by her nickname. But they just smile, all quiet.

"I'm Jack," the third boy says, then points to the shortest one. "This is Zeke and then Flynn."

The blue-eyed kid waves with two fingers.

"They invited us to a party at their rental house tonight," Pita explains. "A bunch of their friends will be there."

"Yeah, it's going to be fun," Jack says.

Pita knows this involves two things I've sworn off—hanging out with tourists, and guys in general—so I'm annoyed she seems so enthusiastic. She doesn't have as much dating experience as I do, and I get that she doesn't want to go to college a virgin, but also . . . what's the point of hooking up with one of these guys when they'll be gone in two days anyway? Did she learn nothing from what happened to me? Doesn't she see the risks?

"We'll be there," she says.

She's still sitting on the blanket, propped on her elbows,

staring up at them. It's a power move, that she didn't even bother to get up to talk to them. I have to respect it. At least a little.

"Cool," Zeke says. "Like ten."

"Cool," Pita says.

Then they walk off, up the beach, laughing about something, though I can't hear what. I settle down next to her, letting my body collapse into the blanket, loving the feeling of the rocks beneath it—the way they press into my back. I don't say anything because I don't have to.

"What? I need a wingwoman," Pita says.

"Why does it have to be me?"

But that's a stupid question. We both have other friends, but none of them are what Pita is to me, or what I am to Pita. We're always each other's first call, each other's forever plus-one. We've known each other since fourth grade.

"My dad won't actually let me go," I say. "Definitely not after ten. That's like four a.m. to him. I'm going to have to sneak out."

"It wouldn't be the first time . . . Please?"

Pita leans down, staring at me, smiling with those perfect Crest Whitestrip teeth, her hands tucked under her chin in this cute little gesture. I love her so much it's ridiculous.

"Okay," I finally say, my face smushed against the blanket. "Okay."

It looks like I'm going to break all my own rules tonight.

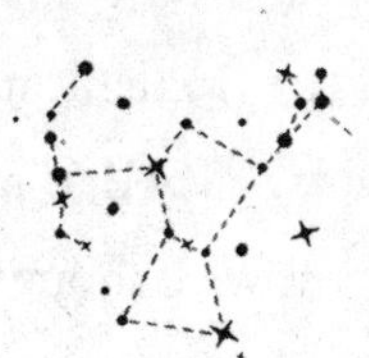

THREE

"The lights, the lights!" I hiss as soon as Pita's golf cart pulls up in the driveway.

They're practically beaming into my dad's bedroom window. She fumbles with them, leaning her head to the side, trying to see the switch in the dark. Finally they're off, and I climb into the passenger side. It takes another minute before she pulls a U-turn out of there.

"Next time I'll roll up incognito," she says.

"There won't be a next time."

"You sure about that?" she says, and smiles.

Maybe my outfit is giving me away. As much as I wanted to wear my sweats and a ponytail, my optimism got the best of me and I did my hair and put on makeup. I have this vintage oversized denim jacket I love and I'm wearing it over my black slip dress, with my beat-up Doc Martens. I look like someone who is excited to go out . . . and maybe I am, just a little bit?

I mean, it's been a while.

My dad has had me on lockdown for almost two months now. I thought it would loosen up after graduation, but he still wants me home every night by ten. He insists I need to focus on *me*. Exploring different options for school or finding a hobby I'm passionate about. He even suggested I go to therapy, which was really weird and kind of out of left field for someone like him—he's never talked to a therapist. Ever.

I know the subtext is: Stay away from boys and girls and romance in general. Don't get caught up drinking or hanging out late when you still haven't figured out what your next steps are. When it came time to apply to schools, I couldn't get it together to write my essays, and while everyone kept telling me I needed to at least get a draft down, and then fill out the paperwork online, I couldn't actually bring myself to do it. Or anything, really. It felt impossible to concentrate on anything for long periods of time. I didn't even really care then if I went to college at all.

"Thank you for coming with me," Pita says in a long, low rasp. "I love youuuuuuu."

"You're welcome."

"I just can't go to college without at least, like, getting naked with a guy. I hooked up with Aaron Klein, like, three times. I barely gave him a hand job."

"You gave eighty-five percent of a hand job," I say. "And that's more than enough. He told David he was thrilled you even considered it."

At that, I can see her fighting off a smile. Pita and I both grew up really Catholic, and I think she's still a little tethered to all the purity and chastity stuff, if I'm being honest. Me . . . not as much. My family stopped going to church after my mom died. She was the one who was into it, and I think my dad really resented the "everything happens for a reason" and "she's with God now" narrative they were pushing on us. I've always felt like you could make up a reason for anything, if you really needed one. That didn't mean it was actually there.

Sometimes bad shit just happens. And it sucks.

The end.

"I just want more experience," Pita says. "I don't want to keep feeling like I'm behind."

"You're not behind."

"But still."

"Experience isn't all it's cracked up to be," I say. "I mean, this past May was a lot of experience for me. Too much, really. And I wish it had never happened."

Pita's expression changes, her mouth suddenly pressed into a hard line.

"We're not talking about you right now," she finally says.

"I didn't mean to hijack the conversation . . ."

"We're talking about me," she goes on. "What *I* want."

"I know, I know," I say.

We round the corner onto Crescent Avenue, which is bustling with tourists. There are all the golf cart rental places, Lloyd's candy shop, the usual restaurants, bars, and stores. There's a sign in the window of one of the beachy boutiques that says CRUISE SHIP SPECIAL: 10% OFF! I have to duck my head to avoid saying hi to anyone. It seems like half our high school works at the places on the water.

Pita takes us all the way down Crescent and turns up Whittle, one of the residential streets off the main drag. The farther we go the quieter it gets, lights twinkling in living room windows. But then we see it up ahead—the modern monstrosity. Its sides are covered in this fake wood material, and there's a balcony up top filled with teenagers.

"*That's* where the party is?"

"I guess . . ." Pita says, then double-checks her texts.

"I always wondered who lived there."

"I guess the answer is no one? They must rent it out."

When it went up last fall, we assumed some celebrity or rich LA person had built it as their summer home. People sometimes set up a place on Catalina, then leave it empty for most of the year until they start visiting again in June. The real estate is already astronomical—completely unaffordable for any normal person—and this just makes it more so. Most of my friends have been living here for generations.

As we get closer, we can hear kids talking and laughing from the roof. In the front window, I can see empties lining the kitchen counter. All it takes is Pita parking and turning off the golf cart for me to feel like this was a bad idea, that I shouldn't be out.

It's just too familiar. It reminds me of what happened

with Harper, of being out and meeting all the wrong people. Then not knowing that I shouldn't trust them.

"Pita! Cal!" I hear a familiar voice call out.

We turn and see Joe Mendoza, a sophomore, coming up the street. For the past four years he's had thick, fluffy hair, with the bangs all wild in the front, but I see he's shaved it for the summer. He's a lifeguard at Descanso Beach Club, so he must've just had it with the heat.

"Right here," he says, waving Pita into a parking spot. He moves his arm in a ridiculous sweeping motion, like he's the valet. "Ease right in. I was saving this for you."

"Aren't you supposed to be the responsible one out of all of us?" I ask, nodding to the brown paper bag he's carrying. I can hear the beer bottles clinking together with each step.

"I am responsible," he says. "The most."

Then as we walk in together, he grabs the bottles out of the bag and it's actually just a bottle of Ketel One and a bottle of Fireball Whisky. The place is massive. It must be four stories, all very sleek and modern, with angular furniture and lots of abstract paintings on the walls. We head up the stairs and into the main floor, where the living room and kitchen are. There must be fifty kids here—a mix of tourists and a few faces I know from school.

"How'd you hear about this?" Joe asks, setting the bottles down on the counter.

He's looking at Pita, hoping she'll acknowledge him, but she's searching for the guys from today, casually scanning the crowd. I spot them before she does—they're sitting on the balcony. They've all got tallboys in their hands.

"Sorry, Joe—we'll have to catch you later," she says.

I almost feel bad for him, she's so nonchalant about it. But then again, I guess if Pita entertained every sophomore guy who had a crush on her, she'd be stuck making small talk for days.

We make our way outside, and Jack and Zeke stand as soon as they see us. They each pull us in for a hug. Flynn's in the middle of talking to a girl who's sitting on a stack of surfboards, and they introduce her as Ingrid. I've never seen her before, so she must be a tourist too, just passing through this weekend. Her jewelry is a bit funky—dangly amber earrings and silver bracelets—which also makes me think she isn't from around here.

"A bunch of these kids are from our senior class," Jack says, gesturing with the can. "We did kind of an unofficial trip. And then we met some of those guys this morning."

He points above us to a second balcony, where another crowd is milling about. They wave down at us, red Solo cups in their hands. Two girls laugh loudly when a third whispers something in their ears.

"When are you in town until?" Pita asks.

"Monday. We're going to try to go snorkeling tomorrow. Maybe check out Shark Harbor, if we can get over there."

"The name is freaking me out, though . . ." Zeke says.

"You should be more afraid of the hike," Pita replies.

"Any recs?" Zeke asks, stepping forward.

I didn't notice earlier, when we first met these guys, but he actually has the cutest face out of all three of them. He has huge eyes and more angular features. He can't be more than 5'7", but Pita's never had a problem with short guys.

"Yeah," she says, leaning in. "You should check out Toyon Bay. It's way cooler than a lot of the places the snorkeling guides recommend. More a local spot."

"Or Lover's Cove," I say, butting in. "Everyone likes Lover's Cove."

Pita scrunches her brows at me. I'm not trying to be an asshole, but she really shouldn't be recommending Toyon Bay to some randos we met five minutes ago. Because it's just that . . . a *local* spot. *For locals*. No one who lives here full-time wants to deal with a bunch of tourists every weekend.

"Do you two want beers?" Jack asks. "There's a ton in the fridge."

"Nah," I say.

But Pita nods. "I'll have one. IPA?"

Zeke says something about Stellas, and with that, he and Pita peel off. To my surprise, Jack goes with them, and when they reach the kitchen island they pull a few beers from the fridge. I watch them through the massive windows, but even once they pour their beers into Solo cups they just stay there, hanging out.

So now I'm stuck with Flynn and Weird Jewelry Girl.

"You two know each other?" I ask them, after an awkward pause.

"I'm here with my family," Ingrid says, and I swear she's got a hint of an accent, though I can't place it. "I'm from Phoenix. We're staying at this place up the road."

"Oh, where?" I ask.

"The Ogygia Inn," she says.

Before I can claim it, Flynn laughs.

"It was all that was left," Ingrid says.

I vaguely remember her parents checking in the other day—a middle-aged couple with a young son and an aggressive hippie vibe. The mom might've actually used the phrase "far out." I never registered Ingrid, though. She must've been off somewhere else.

"That's my dad's inn," I say.

The two of them just stare at me, unsure if I'm kidding or what. I let them sweat it out for a while. But then Flynn says he needs another drink and maybe they should go join the other guys, see what they're up to. I turn, wanting Pita to come save me, to say we can go home because these kids are losers. But I see her and Zeke are already sitting on the couch together, alone. They're talking, beers in their hands.

It's fine. I'm totally fine being alone.

I sit down on the stack of surfboards and cross my legs at the ankles, pretending that I don't care that I'm suddenly all by myself. Joe and some other sophomores are messing around on the upstairs balcony, and I'm sure I could go join them, but also who cares? All these people will be gone in a few days anyway, when all the rooms turn over and they all cash in their return ferry tickets. I'll never see any of them again.

Ten minutes pass, and I check and recheck my phone, scrolling through Instagram and then texting our friend thread, which includes three other girls from school. Pita and I are not as close with them, but still. I say Pita and I decided to go to this house party tonight. **It's that massive house on Whittle Avenue. I bet you could just show up if you wanted**, I write, but I know it's probably pretty obvious that it's a last-minute invitation.

No one responds.

Pita and Zeke have disappeared to another level of the house, and I just assume they're making out. I'm about to get up and join the sophomores upstairs, but then a guy in a Patagonia shell steps out onto the balcony and sits down next to me. He has on a teal Patagonia hat too, but the cloth is faded. He hands me an unopened Red Stripe.

I turn, wondering where he came from. He doesn't look like any of the guys Jack and Zeke were hanging out with. How many kids were with them? Where did they say they went to school again?

"You look really familiar," he says. "Have we met?"

"I don't think so," I say, though there's always the possibility he came through the inn at one point or another. "Is that your best pickup line?"

"Who says I'm picking you up?" He squints at me, all skeptical.

"Why else would you bring a random girl a beer?"

"Like I said, you don't feel random to me."

I crack it open, because a free beer is a free beer, and cheers him. It feels nice going down. I haven't had one in so long. . . .

"I'm Brett."

He holds out his hand and I give it a quick shake. He's attractive, but in that standard hot-guy way. Like, I'm sure he gets with a lot of girls just by smiling and using the same uncreative pickup lines on every single one.

"Callie."

"What's that short for?"

"Calypso."

"Like the myth."

"Like the myth."

"A really pretty name for a really pretty girl," he says.

"Another very original line," I say, and this time, I roll my eyes. Does he think I'm going to fall for this? How many girls has this worked on?

"Oh, come on, you know you are."

I can feel myself softening. Taking in the feel of his muscular thigh pressing against the side of mine. His lips are fuller than most guys', and they're really red—probably from spending all day in the sun. His curly hair peeks out at the sides of his baseball cap. He smells like a campfire, even though there's none here.

"I only have a week left on Catalina," he says.

"What are you doing talking to me, then?"

"I'm looking to get into some trouble."

"I am definitely not the person for that," I say.

But I can feel the tug. I can be a bit impulsive, especially in matters of love. I spent the past two years hanging out with different tourist boys who came through—for a month, for a weekend. I met a cute boy named Lucas who was the lead in an indie band that played all over Portland. I went on two dates with a gamer kid from San Francisco, who was so pale he got horribly sunburned in the strangest places. I used to want to kiss and hang out with all the guys I could. I used to be down for trouble . . . I want to be still. Brett's cute and it would just be a hookup—it might even be good for me to just, I don't know, *kiss* someone else? Try to forget about everything that happened?

Not everything has to be so serious.

"Well, Callie," he says, and when he leans closer, I can tell he's been drinking way longer than I have. Like maybe all afternoon. "That is not what I heard."

He's still trying to be all cutesy about it, but it's obvious there's something more there. I remember how he introduced himself . . . how he thought I was familiar. Is he messing with me, or does he know? Did he somehow see it?

"What do you mean, *that's not what you heard*?"

I stand and brush the sand off my skirt, just to get some space between us. He shrugs, then takes another sip of his beer.

"Are you serious right now?" I ask.

But still, he doesn't answer. And I don't care if he meant it or not. I set my beer down and start walking away.

"Awwww, come on," he mutters. "I was just joking. Come back. Hang."

"I'm good, thanks."

"Suddenly you're a prude," he calls after me. "Please. You're like one step away from a cam girl. Half of Los Angeles saw that photo."

He might as well have punched me. I feel the words with every inch of my body, and they threaten to double me over. I'm suddenly back there, back to April, when I saw the first text in my phone. **I don't know how to tell you this but I think I saw a photo of you. Some guys at Hawthorne Winfield were showing it around.**

I don't turn around or argue because I don't want him to see my face or be in my presence even a minute longer than he already has been. I'm already thinking through everything I did and didn't say to him, if I gave anything away. Pita is somewhere in this house, and I walk inside, toward her, telling myself when I find her it'll be okay. I'll be okay.

One foot in front of the other.

Keep moving forward. Don't look back.

With every step I put between us I feel a bit calmer. The house is hot and sticky with the smell of people and spilled liquor. A group of girls in sundresses crowd around the L-shaped couch. He's not following me, and that at least is a good sign. But all the bad memories are flooding in . . . and I can't stop them. . . .

Harper and I had been texting a little bit after he left

Catalina. I could feel him pulling away, and instead of just letting him go, I took it as some kind of personal referendum. Like it meant something about me. I mean, how could I not take it personally? What's more personal and intimate than giving someone a blow job? Or letting them go down on you? And then they just . . . kind of . . . lose interest?

I wasn't prepared.

I didn't want us—whatever we were—to be over. And besides, every time I stopped texting, he would eventually reach out again, like he didn't want it to be over either. So I don't know why, but when I was on the beach alone one day I took a photo of myself without my bathing suit top on. I thought it was kind of sexy and tasteful—you could only really see one of my boobs; the other was covered by my arm, which I'd tucked in tight to my body. I made this cute, pouty smile and hit send.

And that's it. That's all it was.

That was the beginning and end of everything.

When I finally find Pita, she and Zeke are sitting in the golf cart, talking. They're nuzzling their faces together, all in each other's necks and stuff. Her hair is a little messy in the back, like they've been making out for a while.

"We have to go," I say, and it's not until I stop walking that I realize my hands are shaking. My legs too. I feel like I'm freezing, every inch of my body rocking with cold.

"Are you okay?" she asks.

"No," I say. "Please . . . can we go now?"

FOUR

THREE DAYS BEFORE ODIE

It's after midnight and I'm not even fully in the golf cart yet when a slew of profanities are already spewing from my mouth. When we're finally driving and I can slow my thoughts, an aching, horrible feeling takes hold in the pit of my stomach.

"I could sue him," I say. "I could sue Harper. It's pornography. It's technically child pornography, because I took that photo when I was seventeen. He isn't legally allowed to show it to anyone. What he did was against the law."

Pita drives in silence, her eyes on the road. A whole world is rolling past beside me—people eating ice cream, people shopping for souvenirs in the few shops that are open late, people laughing and having fun—but I can't take any of it in. It's like me, Pita, and that Hawthorne Winfield loser, Brett, are the only three humans on this entire island.

When did that guy see the picture? Did he know it was

me as soon as I walked into that house? Did he just assume I was a slut because of the selfie?

"Harper obviously showed him that picture of me," I say again. "He saw that picture."

"I know, Callie," Pita says.

She seems sad. Quiet.

"Do you think he's still showing people?" I ask. "Do you think it's online somewhere?"

Even the thought makes my throat tighten. Of course I've gone through this over and over again, as if thinking and rethinking it could deliver answers. I've even looked on some porn sites, worried I'd see myself there and wondering if maybe it was only a matter of time before the photo appeared. It's like this one image of me has completely perverted the real me—who I really am. Now I'm just some topless girl on a beach.

"I don't know," Pita says. "I really don't know."

"That picture is the male equivalent of a boner picture," I say. "Not even a dick pic. A picture of a guy in shorts with a boner. That's how innocuous it would be if I were a boy. But somehow, just the fact that it's a selfie and I dared send it to someone . . . that I dared make this cute little smile at the camera . . . it makes me a total whore."

"No one thinks that. . . ."

"I'm allowed to take a pretty photo of myself with my top off," I say. "I sent it to someone I thought I could trust. I really liked him."

We turn up toward the inn, and Pita cuts the lights before we even come close to the front parking lot. She pulls into an open spot and we just sit there, listening to each other's breaths.

"When is this going to end?" I ask. "It's been two months. And it still feels like something I can't outrun. Like . . . am I just going to be this one photo, this topless slut, forever?"

"No," Pita says. "It's not going to go on forever. This was just bad luck, running into someone Harper knows. It was just bad luck."

"I could sue him," I repeat, but the words hold less conviction this time.

I didn't know it last summer, but Harper Thorne is the son of Jason Thorne, one of the founders of TechLook. It's this AI company that has different writing products—systems to make corporate communications easier. They can mimic a CEO's voice, write press releases, draft company-wide emails. They went public last year and he made billions of dollars. That's not an exaggeration . . . literal billions.

As much as I wanted to believe in justice and fairness and all that, when I brought up suing Harper to Matty, he admitted that that would be hard . . . because the Thornes would just try to bury my dad and me financially. They could countersue, or just drag everything on and on so that by the end of it we'd be drowning in legal fees. Matty was the only one who was honest with me about it—I actually couldn't sue Harper for what he did. There was no recourse. Because the inn was failing, and we didn't have the money to do so.

"I hate this," I say. "I hate how powerless it makes me feel."

"I'm sorry," Pita says, but there's a hint of exhaustion in her voice. I know we must've talked about this for, like, five hundred hours at this point, but I don't think I can stop. Not when it keeps feeling like I'm still being victimized, like this is the picture that won't go away.

"I'm sorry too," I say. "That I interrupted everything with . . ."

I search for the boy's name, but can't even remember it. It's like the thing with Brett has eclipsed everything, wiping the rest of the night clean.

"Zeke. He's really sweet."

"He seems really sweet."

I want to be excited about Zeke, about Pita making out with anyone, but I'm having a hard time mustering any kind of enthusiasm for the male species right now. It takes every-thing in me not to say something snarky about guys and hooking up. Or to warn her that there's no way this is going anywhere good . . . she barely even knows him.

"He's here for two more nights, so maybe I'll see him again." Pita runs her hand through her hair, loosening some of the wavy pieces around her face. "He's cool."

"You should. See him again."

I pull the denim jacket closer around me, steeling myself against the wind ripping off the water. There's a small smirk at the corner of Pita's lips, and I can tell she's totally thrilled. I really want to be thrilled for her too.

She's always focused on school and extracurriculars. Field hockey and varsity track and Spanish Honor Society. Her whole family goes to St. Catherine's every Sunday for the ten o'clock mass—they have their usual pew and everything. And when Pita was done with Sunday school, she started helping out there, assisting the teacher with the younger kids. I guess what I'm trying to say is that Pita has always been the opposite of me, in the sense that she always does everything *right*.

If she wants to hook up with a cute guy this summer, and get some experience before she goes off to college so she doesn't feel intimidated on campus . . . then fine. I get it. I just have to keep all my complicated feelings about love and boys out of it.

"This is good. I'm happy for you," I lie, hoping it sounds sincere.

Then before we can get into it any more than we already have, I hug her and climb out of the golf cart. I want to let her enjoy tonight, even if I didn't. I really want to think that what happened to me was a one-off, that so many guys are really nice and kind and wonderfully considerate and respectful . . . that we aren't all doomed.

"This is so exciting!" I call as she drives away.

But my voice sounds too cheerful. Even I don't believe it.

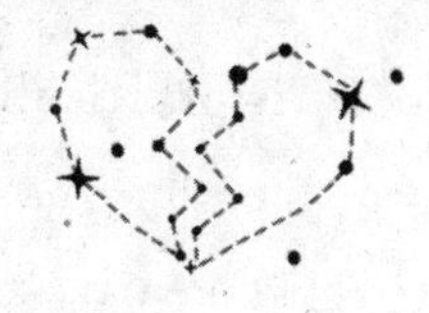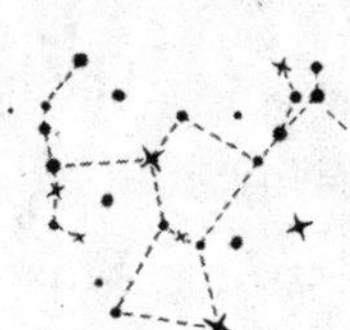

FIVE

THE NIGHT I MET ODIE

I'm supposed to be polishing silverware. Then after I'm done polishing the silverware that I'm not polishing, I'm supposed to wipe down the water glasses in the dining room so that each one is sparkling—not a single gray dishwasher splot anywhere. Lately my dad has become convinced that not having dishwasher splots on the glasses might move the needle with our Yelp rating, just like last week he was convinced Matty cutting his bangs would take us to the next level. The week before it was not having any sand in the lobby; the week before that he made me hand press our Ogygia Inn jackets. He's absolutely forbidden me from telling him to relax and chill, so I just nod and pretend that we can bail out the sinking ship that is our Yelp rating. That we can still, against all odds, turn things around.

I'm supposed to be ticking through all those chores, but instead I'm in the kitchen working on my stuffed cupcake recipe. The hotel lobby is practically deserted at night any-way, and a rainstorm blew in this afternoon—sudden and strong. Most guests retired early, some even borrowing our Ogygia ponchos to go to their rooms, since the rain was coming at them sideways. I just put the little silver bell out in case anyone needs me.

My latest invention is homemade chocolate ganache cupcakes with cookie dough stuffing. I'd just eat the filling as is, because it's impossible to care about salmonella when you're eating raw cookie dough, but I realized other people might not like taking that risk with every bite. I started doing eggless cookie dough, and now I'm experimenting with add-ing in extra butter and a little cream to turn the dough into something a little closer to a custard. I try not to use too much from the pantry, because my dad keeps a pretty close eye on our supplies. Lately, though, I've convinced him that we could use my cupcakes as a perk for guests—to apologize when something goes wrong (room keys that don't work, a later check-in than they wanted), or as a departing gift after an extended stay. We've been doing that for the last month and everyone seems pretty thrilled when a massive cupcake miraculously appears in their hands.

I've lined up all twelve cupcakes on the shiny steel prep table. I use a paring knife to hollow out the center of each one, then put the little coned pieces aside. Then I pipe in my filling one by one. I'm about to plug them all up when I hear the bell ding . . . then ding again.

And again.

Then, like, five times in a row. I can barely get my apron off and get back to the lobby before it starts up again.

"Yes, hello," I say, putting on my best fake smile. It's the workaholic dad who checked in this morning. He had a set of blond twins who looked about three, and a wife who was at least a decade younger than him. He has a plastic trash bag wrapped around his laptop and is otherwise soaked.

"I have a very important email I need to send out to-night," he says, unfolding the laptop in front of me, "and I'm having trouble with the Wi-Fi."

He says it in a way that makes me think he rehearsed it on his walk up the side stairs to the lobby. I smooth my hands over the desk in front of me and smile, trying to present a sense of serene inner calm. Over the past three years I've got-ten a lot better at "customer service." At enduring rudeness or outrageous requests and pretending it's all normal, so that everything at the inn can continue on without any more one-star Yelp reviews.

"So the Ogygia Inn is a TV- and Wi-Fi-free zone," I say, trying to think of the exact words my dad uses when he ex-plains this. "We advertise it that way because we want our guests to relax, unwind . . . and unplug. We want people to lose all sense of time here. We like to think it's a really good thing."

We. Everything is we, my dad used to coach me that first year, when I'd go all deer-in-headlights at confrontation.

But the guy's still glaring at me, watching my every move. As if on cue, the wind gusts open one of the front doors. I walk over and pull it shut. It's only then that I notice how extreme the storm has gotten. The wind has knocked over some of the patio chairs outside. Beyond the railing, I can see the swells are much bigger than usual.

The man waits to respond to me until I'm back at the desk. When I return, he leans one arm on the counter and slouches, like he's preparing to be there for a long while. I can tell he's gearing up . . . and settling in. "So you're telling me you don't have Wi-Fi. How do you text all your girlfriends?"

I hate the phrasing, how he says *girlfriends* like I'm this silly little girl, gossiping into the night. His sideburns are speckled gray . . . he can't be more than fifty-five, but it makes him seem ancient. Like someone's grouchy grandpa.

"I have Wi-Fi at home, in my apartment, but not here at the inn," I say calmly. "I don't text my friends while I'm at work."

It's only partially true. My dad and I have a large two-bedroom apartment behind the lobby—it used to be two of the bigger suites. They were converted in the late nineties, before my parents moved in. I can pick up our apartment's Wi-Fi signal from the front desk and the kitchen, and our desktop computer is hooked up to it—it's how we check everyone in. I'm never really without it. It's only on our deck, overlooking the ocean, or outside, beyond the parking lot, where the service totally cuts out.

"You don't text your friends at work," he repeats, but before I can even respond he rolls his eyes. "I find that really hard to believe."

"There's a great café just a short ten-minute walk away," I say. "On the main street, right by where the ferry lets off. It opens at eight tomorrow morning. They have very reliable internet. Great coffee too."

"I'd like to send it tonight," he says.

Then he just stares at me, his mouth a straight line. But the slight softening (I'd *like* to) tells me I'm going to win this. He's starting to cave, even if it's subtle. His wife obviously chose this hotel so they could have family time together. She's probably furious he's out here, arguing with me, when he could be cuddled up on the couch of their one-bedroom suite, spending quality time with her.

"I understand, but unfortunately there's nothing I can do," I say, and soften the words with a smile—the kind that usually makes guests forget they were mad at me in the first place. "Why don't you relax for tonight. The storm will make doing anything difficult anyway. We can revisit this all in the morning."

He lets out a deep breath, like he wants me to do more.

"If you could just give me a moment," I say. "Just one . . ."

Then I slip back through the kitchen door, revisiting my cupcakes. It takes no time for me to cap two of them and then pipe a warm ganache frosting on top. I put them both in one of our plastic clamshell take-out containers, then decorate them with a few edible flowers I bought from the farmers market. When I bring them back out, I genuinely am smiling.

"Here's a little treat for you and your wife," I say. "Please accept them in lieu of us having Wi-Fi. Tomorrow morning, if you like, I can run you down to the café in the golf cart."

"Fine, thank you," he says, all stern-like. "Chocolate actually *is* her favorite."

But he's softening. I swear I see him fighting back a smile.

"Umbrella?" I ask, pulling one of the Ogygia Inn–branded umbrellas from behind the desk. But he just shakes his head.

He wraps his laptop back up in the clear trash bag, which looks kind of like the extra ones we keep under the guest room sinks. Then he stacks the plastic clamshell on top of it and mutters a thank-you before he leaves, pushing back out into the night.

I watch him go, feeling the slightest bit of satisfaction. I used to hate the night shift. It was like this strange witching hour, where all the grumpiest adults would throw their tantrums. Noises coming from the next room? Tantrum. The hot water wasn't hot enough? Tantrum. Thread count on the sheets not high enough? Tantrum.

But I've finally figured out a way to manage these guests and keep my self-esteem in the process. That isn't an easy feat.

The lights flicker, and the front door gusts open again. It's times like these when the inn feels the loneliest—like it is its own little island on an island. Because there are no other hotels on the south tip of Catalina, the ocean stretches out in front of us for miles. With the exception of the few lampposts on the road below, and the glow that comes off the lobby, the rest of the hill is dark. I figure even though I'm not finished icing all the cupcakes, I should go onto the deck and drag the chairs back against the wall, just in case. Even my dad and Matty weren't prepared for how windy it got tonight. The forecast predicted a rainstorm, not a torrential downpour.

I grab one of the spare ponchos we keep in the closet, then go outside and pick up one of the overturned chairs from the deck. The rain is coming down so hard it stings my cheeks and arms and every other sliver of exposed skin it comes in contact with. The drops are like little razor blades, slicing at everything they touch. I'm stacking the chairs when I see it, out of the corner of my eye—there's an overturned boat floating a little ways offshore.

"No way . . ." I say to myself.

But I'm already starting down the steep deck stairs that zigzag down to the road below. I take them two at a time, to Pebbly Beach Road. I jump down off the pavement and onto the narrow, rocky shore. The water is usually calm here, but the storm has blown in larger swells. Every now and then they rush in, soaking my shoes. I run down the beach until I reach the boat rocking in the waves.

I can't even see the stars behind the clouds, and it makes me feel even more alone than I did before. The boat is so perfectly positioned, right in front of the inn, that it's almost like I was meant to see it. Like I was brought here for a reason, whether I like it or not.

Maybe it's fate, or something like it.

The boat is several yards out. I've never seen it before—it's a racing dinghy. The mainsail has fallen over into the water. It doesn't belong to any of the locals I know, and it doesn't have any of the distinctive markings of the different rental boats on the island. They usually say things like ISLAND RENTALS or CATALINA CHARTER. This is small and sleek, a little silver thing. When I pull out my phone I realize my mistake—I should've gone back into the lobby and called from there. I don't have a single bar.

I'm about to run all the flights back upstairs when I hear a voice, barely audible over the pattering rain. I can't even make out what it's saying, just that it's a fierce, almost primal yell. Everything in me is awake, alert, scanning the ocean. Then I spot the guy, his face visible every now and then, as the boat pitches and heaves in the water.

He's clinging to its side with one hand. He doesn't even have a life jacket on.

And if I don't do something soon, he's going to drown.

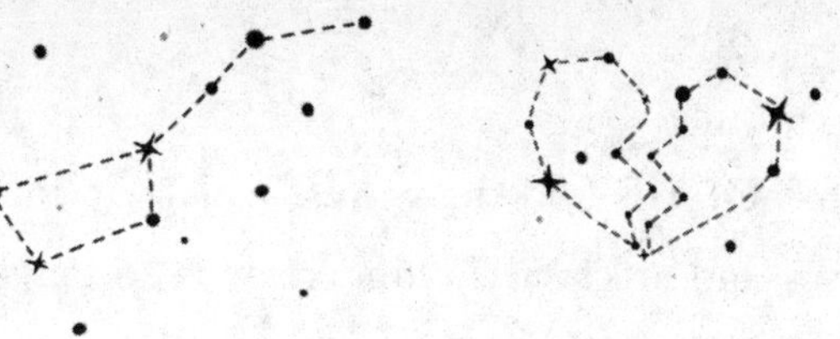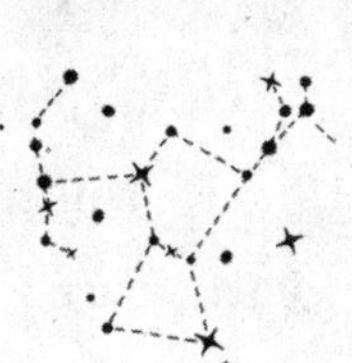

SIX

THE NIGHT I MET ODIE

I turn back to the inn, trying to gauge how long it would take me to get to our apartment on the first floor, in the back of the building, and wake my dad. Get him out of bed, then get back down here, all the while trying to make a 911 call, assuming I can even get service.

The answer is too long.

It would take too long—the guy could slip under in an instant.

The rain is still coming down hard, and the swells are higher than I've seen them in a long while—five feet, maybe more. They're crashing so hard the water runs up onto the road, coating it inky black. I can feel the fear, the way it's hollowing out my body, my limbs numb and cold. And yet . . .

I peel the poncho from my shoulders.

I take off my Sambas and toss them aside, along with my phone.

And then I am running.

Down, through the rocks and the waves, which rip forward, over my calves and ankles. The undertow is so fierce it's hard to stay standing very long. Instead I take a few more running steps until the water is deeper, up to my waist. Then I plunge underneath, trying to escape the current.

The push and pull is stronger than I've ever felt it. It takes so much energy for me to cut through each wave before it crashes, and it seems like as soon as I get my head above water another wave is ripping toward me, ready to pummel me back to the beach. I can just see the boat ahead, rocking in the deeper waters. The man is holding on to the hull, but his hand keeps sliding off it.

"I've got you!" I yell. "Hold tight!"

His head jerks back just enough that I can tell he heard me, that he at least knows I'm there. But just that small moment—me calling to him—throws off my rhythm. A wave crashes over me, pulling me down into the washing-machine churn of the water, and it feels like forever before I can get back up. I already know I'm not going to be able to drag him in alone. The current is too strong, the rain thrashing in my eyes.

I spot the plastic storage chest at the bottom of the stairs back on the shore. The inside is filled with towels and other nonsense we sometimes need for the guests. It has one of those orange lifesaver things on the front of it. I never considered it was for anything more than decoration before now.

I ride the next wave in to the shore, then the next, trying to get back as soon as I can. I sprint up the beach and across the road, then pull the ring free, relieved at how sturdy it feels in my hands. I've seen lifeguards save swimmers before—usually confused tourists who've gotten stuck in riptides or have swum out too far. But they always use those longer foam buoys or the short, squat cans with grips on the side. I don't know how I'm going to do this. It just feels like having some sort of flotation device is infinitely better than trying alone.

Back into the waves, this time holding one of the plastic ropes on the side of the ring. It's cumbersome, but I immediately know it was the right decision. It will give him something to grab on to besides me—a buffer of sorts, so he doesn't panic and drag me down with him. This time I keep rhythm with the waves, ducking under each one before it breaks, and popping up for air just fast enough to get a full breath.

It isn't long before I'm out where the water is rocking, bobbing. Here the whitecaps aren't as fierce, but the swells are enough to make you sick. I keep cutting against the current, doing the crawl stroke with one arm and clinging to the ring with the other. Each time a wave comes, it raises me up up up, then plummets me down, and have to start swimming all over again.

As I get closer to the sailboat I anticipate another problem—it's just a dinghy, but it's big enough that if a sudden swell comes and knocks it sideways, it would be over. I'd be done. It's upside down, the carbon fiber body completely out of control. It could pummel me.

"You have to swim!" I yell. "I'm close—just try!"

The guy turns his head again, and I can tell he hears me, that he knows I'm close. He seems disoriented, his black hair clinging to the front of his face, covering his eyes. A dry bag tied to the side of the boat bobs along beside him, just out of reach. If the water were even a little bit calmer I could just throw the ring to him, but it's too much of a risk. It could be swept off.

He turns away from the boat and slips into the water. He doesn't put up much of a fight. His arms flail this way and that, and then when he can't swim any further, he disappears under a large swell. As soon as he reappears, I move in, grabbing him around the shoulders.

He's so much heavier than I anticipate. I cling to him as best I can, but I have to keep adjusting, and he slips from my grasp. The whole ocean surrounds me, ready to swallow us both up.

"Hold this, hold on," I yell, and then try to maneuver the ring under his arms.

I swear I hear him muttering thank-yous, but all I can think about is how I'm going to get him through the waves and to the beach. I lean all my weight back and kick as hard as I can with my legs. I can't really hold on to him so instead I hold on to the plastic rope on the side of the ring.

I kick and kick, but it's like the water is cement. I'm not

even sure if we're moving. The rain is stinging my eyes, and I've never been more grateful than when we finally reach the breaks, because I know the waves will help us from here.

"You have to hold tight," I yell against the rain. "Hold tight to this rope."

I cover his hand with my own, hoping he has enough strength left to just keep the ring close. He has a thin jacket on but there's no way to tie him to the ring, so instead I help thread one of his wrists through the rope loop on the side. Then I kick some more, until the first massive wave takes us rolling over its top.

It comes hard and fast, and I try to use it to carry us as far to shore as possible. I kick and use my free hand to paddle, but then a second wave follows and I'm completely lost. It's all I can do to hold on to the side of the ring. I keep kicking, even when I'm underwater. But the currents are too strong. I lose my grip and the ring slips away, out from under my fingers.

I'm churning, tossed in the waves. Another wave hits and soon I feel the rocks beneath me, how they shift underfoot. I struggle, another wave catching me from behind. It takes a while for me to get my bearings in the shallows. The rain is still pelting down, relentless. When I search the shore I see the guy is now face down in the water, the ring floating away from him.

He's unconscious now—he must've taken in water. I get his head out but he's so heavy, and I'm exhausted. I drag him as best I can up onto the beach, but we're still at the edge of the water when I flip him over. I smack his cheeks and try to shake him awake. Nothing works.

"Help! Someone help!" I scream up at the inn. It towers above us, the light from the lobby blurry in all the rain. It feels so far away and the storm is so loud.

"We need help!" I yell again.

I get under his arms and manage to get him a little farther onto the sand. I took a CPR class two years ago, when I was convinced I wanted to be an EMT, but I've never had to use anything I learned. His chest isn't moving, though. If I don't do something, he might not make it.

I feel for a pulse but it's hard and confusing in the cold—I think I feel one but I'm not certain. I tip his chin up and back, hoping that will free up the airway. I've heard sometimes it only takes that for someone to spit up and come to.

As I reposition him, some of the hair falls back away from his face. I can tell now he's not some guy or some man—he's a boy. He can't be much older than I am.

"Come on," I say, and give him some quick smacks on the cheeks and chest. "Wake up!"

It's not working. Nothing's working.

I pinch his nose and then cover his mouth with mine and start breathing my breaths into his lungs. The quick one two, one two, steadies me. I keep doing that, giving him short, one-second puffs of air. I don't know how long it takes, but suddenly he sputters.

He turns over, coughing, his back heaving with the effort. He falls forward onto his hands, his fingers gripping the rocks. He's puking a little bit but he's okay. He's going to be okay.

I let out a sweet, relieved laugh.

"You're alive," I say, not knowing who I'm even talking to. But the relief is already turning into something bigger, bolder, every inch of my body thrilled that we've both escaped.

We're here now, on the shore. Safe.

"We made it," I say. I throw my arms around his shoulders. I hug him close, our cheeks pressed together. Then I squeeze my eyes shut, letting his breaths calm me.

SEVEN

THE NIGHT I MET ODIE

When I pull back, I see he isn't just a boy my age, he's a ridiculously cute boy my age. Even in the pouring rain, even with the terror of the night still coursing through me, it's undeniable. He's staring up at me with these dark brown eyes, his lashes thick and wet. His dimples are so pronounced that they're noticeable even when he's not smiling. And then there's his chest, so ropy and muscular I can feel it through his jacket.

I'm suddenly self-conscious. I roll off him and brush my hair away from my face, instead focusing on his boat, which is caught in the breaks now. With each wave it comes closer to shore. It's a lightweight racing boat, the kind that can rip around the ocean. I've seen people take them up to thirty miles an hour or more. They're for beautiful days, days of fun and relaxation—I can't figure out why anyone would take one out in this weather.

He tries to sit up, but with every movement he winces.

He's holding his hand to his back, and I can already see a dark spot spreading out near the bottom of his jacket—it looks like blood. His eyes squeeze shut.

"We need to get you to the hospital," I say.

I stand, searching the beach for where I dropped everything. My shoes, my phone . . . it's hard to see anything in the dim light. There are only a few lampposts along the road—barely enough to see.

"What's your name?" I ask. "I can get my dad, he can drive us. We have a first aid kit up at the inn, and towels—we can call whoever you need us to. Your parents must be worried."

He pulls up the sleeve on his jacket, and I can see there's another cut along his forearm. I'm about to kneel down and help him when the boat crashes into the shore a few yards away from us, the battens mangled on the rocky shore. The sailcloth is torn, which makes me think he wrecked on a bigger rock before the boat capsized.

"I don't need you to call my parents," he says.

He's cradling his arm now as he stands, but I can tell he's still disoriented from the wreck. I inch closer to his side, anticipating he might fall.

"We have to," I say. "You could've died out there. You could have a concussion. Your arm might be broken or—"

"My arm isn't broken," he says, and it comes out a little short.

I wonder what happened to the grateful version of this person, the one who muttered thank-yous as I dragged his sad, exhausted body all the way in to shore. It's like he's already forgotten what just happened. That I risked everything to save him.

"Don't worry about me," I say sarcastically. "Really. I am okay. Totally fine after nearly drowning, trying to bring you in. What were you doing on that thing anyway? Are you out of your mind?"

"The weather turned," he says. "I didn't know there was going to be a storm."

"Why weren't you wearing a life vest?"

"I had one on the boat . . . I lost it."

"You have to wear them, that's kind of the point. It doesn't do any good if it's just tied to the mast."

"I know that. Obviously."

We stare at each other, and I'm immediately annoyed at his tone. He seems defensive, when all he should be is grateful. Even the way he's standing right now, his arms crossed, his shoulders raised in the slightest shrug, is offensive.

"Oh, and you're welcome," I shoot back. "Really. You don't have to keep thanking me."

"Thank you," he says. "I thought I said thank you."

"This was reckless. You could've gotten yourself killed."

"I didn't mean to."

"It doesn't matter."

Now he's looking past me, over my shoulder, to the spot on the beach where his boat washed ashore. It's tipping back and forth, the torn sail catching in the wind.

"Please," he says. "Can you just help me drag my boat in?"

"What?"

"If my parents find out what happened, I'm going to be in so much trouble. I'm already in so much trouble. I don't want to be in any more."

"I hate to break it to you . . . but I don't see a way for you to lie about this . . ."

"I just have to right it," he says. "Maybe I could wait out the storm here. Then I'll sail straight back."

This boy is deluded.

What does he even mean by "here"? On the beach, in the rain? At the inn? And what about my dad? Does he not realize that I have my own parent to answer to? One who is already fundamentally opposed to me hanging out with guys this summer? I already jumped into the ocean for this kid . . . now I'm supposed to host him for the night?

What the actual fuck?

"If we could just get it onto the beach . . . I could fix the sail . . ."

"The beach?"

"Please? Help me move it?"

I'm about to tell him how absolutely unhinged this all is, but he is already taking off across the shore. The racing boat is light—it can't be more than sixty pounds—but it's pitiful, watching him drag it by himself. He heaves it over the rocks, but he has to actually wade back into the shallow water to push the bottom of it out.

"Get out of there," I say. "What are you thinking?"

I wave him onto shore and when he gets up, we both pull the stern up together. There's a dry bag tied to the side and he pulls it off and starts digging through it. Everything in it is soaked. Still, he hangs an extra shirt over his shoulders and retreats farther up the beach, dragging the boat behind him.

"We have to hide it," he says, though I don't know why he thinks we're a team all of a sudden. "Where can we hide it?"

There's a little crest in front of us, where the beach technically ends. Just on the other side it's more secluded. There's a few warehouses down the road, and no one really goes back there to swim or walk. I point him in that direction and we drag the boat together.

When we finally set it down, he positions it so it makes the tiniest one-person shelter. Just enough to protect him from the wind and the rain. Then he tucks himself underneath. He's shivering, holding his arms around his body, hugging himself.

"Please don't tell anyone I'm here," he says. "Please. I'm literally begging you."

There's a thin, fragile quality to his voice, like he's trying not to cry. I don't want to feel anything for him, for this boy who I don't know and who is being quite rude, considering the circumstances, but I also don't want to send him back to, like, an abusive home or anything. He's acting like his life is in mortal danger.

Is it? How is that even possible?

He's wearing an expensive sailing jacket, from some fancy brand I've seen adults wear.

"You're going to stay here?" I ask. I look around. The rain is still coming down, the water thick and frothy. It'll be hours before the storm clears.

"Why not? I'll be okay."

"It's freezing."

"It's fine. Just don't tell anyone I'm here. I'll head back out as soon as I can."

"Your boat is dented. The sail is ripped."

"The rip isn't that bad."

He looks up at it, as if he's not seeing the same thing I am.

Now I'm really annoyed. He doesn't want to go to the hospital, or call anyone, or even acknowledge this happened. And he wants to sleep outside, in the pouring rain? Like, maybe he could keep his boat here for a few days . . . maybe my dad or Matty wouldn't find it. But if he tries to stay the night out here, he could freeze to death.

The water was sixty-five degrees, at most. We're both completely soaked. With the wind ripping off the waves, it's a real possibility.

"You can't. I didn't save your life so you could die of hypothermia," I say. "Leave the boat here. Just . . . follow me."

When I get over the rocky hill, I glance back up at the inn, half expecting my dad to be standing on the cliff above. But all I see is the light casting out from the lobby windows, turning the rain a golden white.

I climb the stairs on the side of the inn. Because room 2 is the only one on the first floor, it has its own private landing, with a window that faces to the east. You'd never pass it, unless you were trying to get down to the road—but most of the guests head to the beaches off Crescent Avenue or the Descanso Beach Club, which have their own restaurant or bar. My dad never took the lockbox off the side of the door. It takes only four digits to get the spare key and get inside.

Immediately, I'm hit with the musty smell. I open the side window to get some air in. An old plastic-wrapped set of blankets and sheets sits in the middle of the naked mattress.

"You can stay here for the night," I say. "It'll get you out of the cold."

"Thank you, but I don't need—"

"You don't need a place to stay? What are you even talking about?"

"I'll leave tomorrow morning, as soon as the storm clears."

"Even if the storm clears," I say, "it would be really risky to try to take that boat out on the ocean again. The mast is bent. The sail needs repairs. Where were you coming from? The other side of the island?"

He doesn't answer, and I feel a hollowness in my stomach. There's no way . . .

Is it possible he was coming from farther than that?

"I don't want to put you out," he says, but I can see he's faltering.

He's noticed the table and chair in the corner, and he's sitting now. It's stuffy in here, sure, but it's also warm. I bet we still have a pack of towels somewhere.

"This will work tonight," I say. "I can get you a ferry ticket tomorrow."

"I said, I'll just go back on my—"

"We can argue about it tomorrow," I say.

He stands, already reaching for the old sheets. He rips off the plastic and pulls the first blanket out and around his shoulders. He holds it close, completely content with it. He seems thrilled to have something warm and dry.

It's pretty shocking to watch, considering that blanket has been sitting there for . . . years?

He doesn't seem to care.

"Are you hungry?" I ask. "Do you need food?"

"I just need to rest," he says.

Then he lies down on the bed, lying his head flat against the mattress, as if I'm not there. Of course I feel for him— something bad has just happened, and before that, maybe something even worse. I don't know what he's trying to escape or why. But there's a part of me that feels validated . . . because it's true, what I've been feeling these past few years— boys are always bad news.

Even when you save them from a raging ocean.

Even when they're ridiculously cute.

"I'll come by in the morning," I say before leaving. "Don't answer the door to anyone. Don't let anyone know you're here. And please, please don't do anything dumb."

He grumbles a yes, and I shut the door behind me, resting my back against it. The key is freezing in my palm. It hits me all at once that I'm soaked, my shirt and hair sticking to me, the cold of the night finally taking hold. Even though I just saw him, even though all around me there's proof that it happened, it feels like I'm in some kind of strange dream.

What just happened?

What have I just done?

EIGHT

THE FIRST WEEK WITH ODIE

The dining room is bustling with guests. In the past two years we've downgraded our breakfast to continental to give our chef, Lenora (and the budget), a break. The blond twins are in front of the cereal bar. The little girl spins the lever on the Froot Loops all the way to the right and an avalanche of colorful Os come out, pouring down until her mom is able to stop it.

I'm assuming the workaholic father is at the café this morning, sending off whatever important email he'd been going on about last night. Outside, the sky is still gray and drizzly, the raindrops slipping down the windows in long, lazy streams. I grab a blueberry muffin from the tray of pastries and duck back into my dad's office. He has one of those huge oak swivel chairs, and I sit in it and eat, turning back and forth, grateful for the quiet.

It happened, I tell myself. *That really happened.*

Every time I think about last night I feel a sudden swell of pride. That I didn't hesitate—that I just went right into the water to save him. That I was able to, that I was strong enough, despite him being bigger than me and the waves being so fierce. I don't love that he's still here, that I have to keep all of it a secret, but I'd be lying if I said I wasn't a little bit excited.

It's like he's this mystery that needs solving.

I don't even know his name.

What could be so bad that he wouldn't want his parents to know where he is? Or to at least tell them that he's safe? Aren't they worried about him? Where do they think he is?

The blueberry muffin is a little hard, but I choke it down, thinking I can steal at least one or two more pastries from the breakfast table and bring it to him. There's nothing in our apartment, so unless I go out in the rain, that's the only option.

A few years ago my dad and I stopped buying groceries, and instead resolved to just graze at the inn or do takeout when we needed to. It seemed like the easiest, most obvious thing, but I sometimes still open the fridge out of habit. The crusty bottles of ketchup and mustard stare back at me, next to a baking soda box we never bothered throwing away. It feels a little lonely . . . like is it even a home if you only sleep there? If you never invite friends over or have dinner around the kitchen table?

"Callie—I've been calling you." My dad's voice stirs me.

He pokes his head through the door.

"I'm off today," I say. "Didn't you see the schedule?"

My dad looks like he's aged two decades in the past five years. Lines have appeared around his eyes and mouth, and his hair has gone gray on the sides. It must be the stress. Trying to figure out how to stay in the black each month, especially when there's always another winter coming for us, the slow season hovering like storm clouds on the horizon. Even with all the small business loans we took out, we never really recovered from Covid and all those long, empty days when no ferries came through. The island was desolate and everyone was panicked, not knowing if things would ever be better again.

"I just wanted to say hi. Can't I say hi to my daughter?" he asks. "I didn't get to see you this morning."

"Oh, hi . . ."

"Anything unusual happen last night?"

I nearly spit out my muffin.

"What do you mean?"

"It's just . . . I thought I heard someone yelling."

He leans his head on the doorframe. My dad is tall and thin, with twiggy, stick-straight legs. Sometime guests think they can bulldoze him, but he has this steadfast way. He notices everything, and he never does anything he doesn't want to. Right now it feels like he's staring right through me, like he can see my bones.

"Oh . . . no . . ."

"You didn't hear that?" he asks. "You didn't hear some-one yell?"

Part of me wants to tell him. Part of me worries he already knows, and this is a test somehow, to see if I explain what happened. I remind myself: I checked and rechecked the news several times this morning. There was never any mention of a missing boy or a racing sailboat. I couldn't even find a record of a race yesterday. There's no way my dad knows anything, which is for the best, because he'd be furious I didn't immediately run upstairs and tell him what was going on. The fact that I kept the boy in room 2 for the night . . . that I'm essentially *hiding* him . . .

It wouldn't go over well.

Besides, the boy is leaving today—and I don't want to get into it, how there's this kid my age who also happens to be crazy good-looking, and I decided to secretly keep him in our spare room overnight instead of just calling my dad and bringing him to the hospital. I already made the wrong decision—I don't need to get in trouble for it too.

"It was pretty uneventful," I say, then take another bite of my muffin. "The storm was crazy, but other than this guy who gave me a hard time about the Wi-Fi . . . I didn't notice anything weird."

I play with the wrapper on the sides, peeling it off. Tearing it a little.

"Huh. Strange."

"I might go into town today," I say. "Meet Pita."

"Okay—it's your day off. I'm not the boss of you."

"Right now," I laugh, completing our joke.

He comes over and gives me a kiss on the head. He's not a sentimental guy, but occasionally he'll hug me in passing, maybe tousle my hair, like we're a dad and daughter on some Disney Channel show. It feels like his idea of what we should be? Like this approximation of closeness?

I wonder if my mom hadn't died, if we actually *would* be close.

No approximation needed.

As soon as he's gone I toss the rest of my muffin in the trash and go back to the breakfast table, stacking a new plate with croissants and some fruit. We only do apple and bananas with the continental spread, but it's something.

To get down to room 2 I have to go onto the deck and down the stairs, which means I pass Matty on my way out. I try not to make eye contact, but he's already leaning in, wanting to pull me into a conversation.

"Where are you going?" he asks. "What are you up to today?"

"Nothing," I say.

"I thought you hate croissants." He looks at the plate, piled high with pastries. "You said they're too messy, like when you bite into them it makes bread confetti."

"You know . . ." I say. "They're growing on me lately."

"You hear the news?" he asks.

My stomach tightens, and I wonder if something broke

in the last hour, since I last checked. It might've taken a minute for the boy's disappearance to be reported.

"Um . . ."

"Paulie's Seafood Shack is closing," he says.

"Oh no. . . ."

It's an institution on the island, and the all-you-can-eat-shrimp nights are epic, for tourists and locals alike. It's always most fun in the offseason, though, when Paulie's family break out their instruments and use the shack as an open mic of sorts, where all different people can perform live music. Or even just try new stuff out—you never had to be good.

"That sucks," I say, because it does.

"Yeah—Paulie needs a knee replacement. He just doesn't think he can do it anymore."

"Oh wow," I say, and I don't know how to get out of this now without seeming like an asshole.

Thankfully a beat passes, then a guest appears, asking Matty for the spare umbrellas, and if he can get a golf cart to drive them into town. When I'm certain he's fully occupied, I go out onto the deck, which is still empty because of the rain, the chairs still pushed up against the lobby windows. Then I disappear down the side stairs, zigzagging all the way down the building.

The rain is light but enough to wet my face, my hair. By the time I get to the room and get the key from the lockbox, even my tank top is damp.

"Hey—it's me," I say, but I'm already opening the door.

The boy is lying on the bed, a towel around his waist, reading one of the old paperback novels that were left on the shelves. He is not wearing a shirt. The back window is open—all I can see is faint sunlight streaming in over his golden-brown chest, which is just ropy enough but not too muscley to seem like he tries too hard. His hair is much curlier now that it's dry, a big swoop of it falling over his forehead.

He is insanely, undeniably hot.

"Sorry—I should've—" I say.

"It's fine. I'm just trying to fully dry off."

"You must be freezing still."

"It's getting better."

His wet clothes are strung up around the room—hanging over the shower bar in the bath, draped on the wooden chairs by the dresser. His pants from last night are hanging on a hook behind the door. The room doesn't feel as damp and dismal as it did before—something about the daytime makes it almost seem cheerful. I can barely see the puckering dry-wall, the grayish-brown spots on the ceiling. And the cool breeze coming in from the window softens the air. I know I should close it—Matty or my dad might notice it if they come down—but it seems cruel to lock him up in here.

"I brought you some food," I say.

I put the plate beside him and he immediately sits up.

"Thank you . . . and, you know, sorry for being a dick last night," he says.

"You were only seventy percent of a dick," I say.

"Only seventy percent . . . that's not terrible."

"It was just the context."

"Yeah, I guess when someone saves your life you should at least be, like, nice and stuff."

"At least."

He smiles, and those dimples appear in both cheeks. Then he scarfs down half a croissant, mmming under his breath.

I do not want to be attracted to him. I can already feel it clouding things, how of course I want him to stay here, in this room—in that towel—for as long as humanly possible. I want to keep him, like a sweet, sad pet, and come visit him every day for the rest of his life.

"Little light reading?" I ask, picking up the book.

It's one of those cheap romance novels, and it has a girl in a lavender ball gown on the front, a man embracing her from behind. He has his face buried in her neck.

"The only reading. It's not bad, actually."

The first page I open to says something about "devouring his entire being." I set it back down on the mattress.

"My phone's gone," he says, explaining. "It must've slipped out of my pocket last night. And I could use the distraction."

Then he bites into the other half of the croissant, watching me, as if he's waiting to see what I'll say next. What I'll do.

I'm happy I took a shower this morning. I let my hair dry wavy, and my white tank top is cute, with tiny ruffles along the neck. I'm wearing my baggy Levi's but I feel confident . . . like myself. I don't want to be nervous or excited right now—to even be thinking about what I look like or what I'm wearing—but here we are.

"About that . . ." I say. "Are you ready to make some calls? I could take you somewhere on one of the golf carts. Or we could have someone tow your boat for you."

I pull my phone out of my back pocket, hand it to him.

"Are you going to make me?"

"I guess I can't make you . . ."

I'm still standing by the edge of the bed, and it all feels a bit formal, but it would be odd to sit in the chair all the way across the room—like I'm a detective interviewing him or something. And the thought of sitting on the bed, beside him . . . it's just too intimate.

"I know I'm putting you in a weird spot," he says.

"Beyond weird."

"I don't want to." He brings his face up, playing with the swoop of hair by his forehead. "I'm really grateful for what you did. That was . . . pretty incredible. I don't think many people would risk everything for someone they don't even know."

"You don't have to keep thanking me," I say. "Just call your parents. Tell them where you are. It can't be as bad as you think it will be."

At that, his eyes widen, and he just shakes his head. Like I really don't get it.

"It's pretty bad," he says.

"Try me."

"Things are bad enough that I don't really spend time at my house anymore," he says. He's still not looking at me, though, instead focusing on a spot on the bare mattress. His fingers wander over a seam. "I've been spending most days on my boat. I took it out yesterday, but I didn't realize a storm was coming . . . and I was trying to outrun it . . . like I thought maybe I could actually make it to the island before it hit me."

"Where were you sailing from?" I ask, but I'm becoming even more nervous about the answer. His story isn't checking out.

"Los Angeles."

Whaaaaaaat???

"You tried to sail that boat from Los Angeles to Catalina Island," I say slowly, trying to understand. "Seriously. That's basically a dinghy."

"I know, it was stupid. Then I got caught up in the storm."

"That is incredibly stupid."

The sailboat is a foil dinghy, and those are only supposed to go short distances—they're for racing, not open water passage. It's twenty-two miles from Los Angeles to Catalina, all of it over open ocean. It takes a massive ferry over an hour. The boy's boat has no cabin, no GPS, no VHF radio, no lights, no radar reflector. There's nowhere to even store food or supplies. I'm surprised he even had a dry bag on it. If anything goes wrong—and a lot can—there's no way to call for help. The water between LA and Catalina is notorious for its swells. He's lucky he made it as far as he did.

"I can't believe you did that," I repeat. "You can't do that ever again."

"I know."

"Do you?" I ask. "You're lucky to be alive."

"I'm lucky because of you."

Then he looks up, his gaze meeting mine. His eyes are the kind of brown that has golden flecks in it, the color mottled. His expression is serious enough that I can tell he understands this is bad, that he really fucked up. What he did was beyond stupid, and he could've gotten us both killed.

"I was pissed," he says. "I was pissed and I wasn't thinking. I'm sorry you got dragged into it. It's not fair."

"It isn't."

"And I'm not saying this as an excuse," he says. "But, like . . . lately everything is kind of in flux. I was living with my mom and my stepdad, but my stepdad is toxic. We basically hate each other. So then I moved in with my dad, but that came with its own stuff."

"What kind of stuff?" I ask.

"He's just a classic narcissist. Everything has to be his way, and he just sees me as an extension of him. Like I'm one of his employees he needs to manage and control."

He leans forward and sets his head in his hand, working at his hair with his fingers. It doesn't seem like he's lying . . . it's all too specific. Even the whole narcissist thing—I could see how that would make you want to be out of your house all day.

"It sounds shitty," I say.

What I really want to say is I understand, at least a little bit. How it feels to be unmoored. How it feels to have your home not feel like a home. My dad can be strict, and he takes everything way too seriously, especially lately, but he's not a narcissist . . . or toxic.

I honestly don't know what I'd do if he was.

What he's describing feels like emotional abuse, at the very least. If he doesn't feel comfortable being at his dad's place, and he has nowhere else to go because of the situation with his mom . . . that's awful. I feel for him that he has to deal with that.

"I'm not looking for sympathy or whatever," he says. "I'm just trying to explain why I did . . . what I did. It was careless, but also there was other stuff going on."

There's this long, uncomfortable pause, and I want to fill it with something, but I don't know what. If I tell him he can stay, it feels like I'm putting a stamp of approval on something I don't approve of. But how could I tell him to go back to an abusive situation? To parents who don't give a shit? How could I ever feel good about that?

"Maybe we should've started with something simpler," I say. "Like, what's your name?"

He lets out a low laugh, and smiles. "That's a good idea. You go first."

"I'm Callie," I say.

"Hi, Callie."

"Hi."

He smiles again, and I do think this would be easier if he wasn't as cute. It's not exactly a hardship, me having him here for the rest of the day . . . or longer.

"All my friends call me Odie," he says.

"Hi, Odie."

"Hi," he says, and the dimples appear again.

I feel it in my chest, that smile. My face is warm, and it's getting harder to look directly at him. Instead I focus on my hands.

"You can stay here as long as you need," I finally say. "But I'm going to say again, I think you should at least tell your parents where you are. They're probably terrified."

"It's actually not as much of a problem," he says. "Because my dad thinks I'm with my mom for the summer, and my mom thinks I'm with my dad. One of the only benefits of your parents being divorced. You can play them off each other."

"They're going to figure it out eventually."

"You don't know them. They're in their own worlds."

"I'm not supposed to have anyone in here, though," I say. "My dad would be pissed."

"I know, I know. I can take the boat back, I'll just—"

"You can't take the dinghy back, no. I won't let you. Why don't we get you on a ferry?"

"I'm just . . . not ready for that. For a whole thing—then I'd have to find someone to bring my boat back, I'd have to tell my parents. Maybe I can fix the boat. I'd just need a few days—as soon as the weather is better, I'll fix it."

But there's something about the way he says it—it doesn't sound entirely convincing. It's like now that he has somewhere that is not with either of his parents, and not out on the open ocean where his life is constantly as risk, he wants to just camp out. It's not a good idea, but what other alternatives do we have right now? And I'd be lying if I said I didn't want at least another day with him. . . .

I point to the plate, which still has the fruit and a croissant on it. As usual, the mattress is now covered with a spray of bread confetti. Croissants really are a nuisance.

"I'll sneak down some more food later," I say. "Maybe a camping lantern or flashlight? I'm guessing it gets pretty dark in here."

"I was so tired I didn't even notice."

I walk backward toward the door, unsure what to even say at this point. He's not a guest . . . he's not even a friend. For the most part, this person is still a complete stranger. He only became "Odie" a few minutes ago.

"I'll see you in a bit?" he asks, sitting forward.

"Yeah—in a bit," I say. "I have a few things I need to do."

"Right. Sure," he says. "Just one question . . ."

I pause, a little worried about what he's going to ask.

Does he need money? New clothes? Is he going to want to go into town at some point?

"Yeah?"

"Where should I go to the bathroom? The toilet and sink don't work."

"Oh, right . . ."

I'd forgotten my dad turned off the water ages ago, when the leaks started. The room looks normal enough. You wouldn't suspect.

"I guess you could go down to the beach, in the ocean? There's also a coffee shop on the other side of the hill that you could use, but it's a fifteen-minute walk up the road. You'd have to just pretend you're coming in from the beach. Just make sure no one sees you. I can pick up a bunch of bottled water for you this afternoon."

"Thanks."

This already feels like a lot of responsibility—too much. But there's also something kind of exciting about being needed so much, about having this secret. It's like it's me and him here, and the rest of the world is just a formality. Like, sure, I have to go out and see friends and get food and be a person, but how could anything be more important than this? Than trying to keep this real live human boy alive?

I give him this casual, awkward wave as I go. Then I cross the road and cut across the rocky beach until I get to the place where we hid his boat. It's far enough away from everything that you can't see it from the main road, or the beach in general—you'd really have to be searching for it. But we'll have to come up with a better hiding spot once the weather is better and the guests start wandering more. Just one person asking my dad about this could send up red flags.

I'm about to leave when the writing on the hull catches my eye. The racing boat is a Bieker Moth, the brand clearly labeled across the front. It has an elegant white hull that curves up like moth wings. That's why they call it that.

My boat, he'd said. Hadn't he?

An uneasy feeling takes hold in the pit of my stomach.

This boat costs fifty thousand dollars at least.

Which means Odie, poor, sweet Odie . . . is fucking rich.

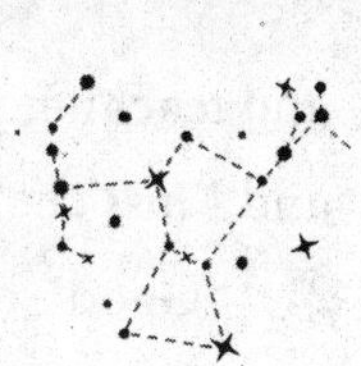

NINE

THE FIRST WEEK WITH ODIE

"The light within me recognizes the light within you," says Thea, our yoga instructor. She presses her hands into prayer position and we all follow, doing the same. "Namaste."

We bow together, honoring her light. I always feel a little silly doing this. Like, is there really a light, and what are we even talking about right now? But I started tagging along to the Sunday yoga class that Pita goes to, and I have to admit, I just feel better after.

Calm. Content.

Thea is about fifty-five, with long gray hair that falls down past her butt. She lives on the other side of the island, so I don't run into her much, but when I do she always asks me a bunch of questions about how I'm doing, then nods and smiles at me like I'm the most fascinating person she's ever met. *She's probably on drugs*, my dad said when I mentioned it. But it's not like that. She's spent enough time meditating and teaching yoga that she's just kind of blissed out. And she and I just click.

"Good seeing you, my loves," she says, giving each of our shoulders a squeeze as we kneel, rolling up our mats. "When do you leave, Pita?"

"Not until the second week of August." Pita snaps the bag straps into place.

"Class won't be the same without you," Thea says. "You'll still come and keep me company, won't you, Callie?"

Thea smiles sweetly at me, her green eyes all twinkly and bright. Of course I want to come, but this is something I do with Pita, and I can't imagine sitting in this room next to some random tourist in neon floral Lululemon. Who would I make eye contact with when Bart, the scuba in-structor from Two Harbors, farts while we're in downward dog? Who am I going to get smoothies with afterward?

"Of course," I lie.

We get more shoulder squeezes, then Sari, who owns two different boutiques on Crescent Avenue, flags Thea down. She wants some tips on how to perfect her crow pose.

"I'm going the juice route today," I say as we step out the door and into the morning sun. "I ate one of the infamous Ogygia blueberry bricks, and I don't think I even have room for a smoothie."

Pita doesn't respond, and when I turn, I see she's on her phone. She's smirking as she texts, and it's like the rest of the world doesn't exist. She practically trips over the curb on our walk up the block.

"So it's going well, huh?" I ask.

"Huh?"

"You're texting with Zeke, right?"

"Is it that obvious?"

"You've been checking your phone all morning. You've barely said two words to me."

Pita tucks it back in her bag. She hasn't mentioned Zeke since the party, and I didn't know if that was because of how spectacularly badly the night went for me, or if he flaked on her. To be honest, I didn't feel like asking. I've been wondering if maybe Zeke and his friends knew that guy Brett—if maybe they were the reason he was there in the first place.

"He's really great," Pita says. "A really good guy."

"You've only known him for a few days. . . ."

"Yeah, but it seems like it." She pulls out her phone again, staring into it like she's possessed. "He's been saying the sweetest things."

"I just wonder . . . do you think he knew that guy? Brett? Do you think they invited him to the party? They said they—"

"What? No," Pita says. "He's not even from LA. Zeke is from Orange County."

I let out a breath. I didn't realize how uncomfortable it was making me, but it's a huge relief to know Pita isn't involved with some shitty guy. When I turn back to her to say as much, her cute, flirty, I'm-texting-with-my-crush smirk is gone. She's staring past me, down at the beach.

"You know . . . I'm going to try to meet up with them," she says. "Catch you later?"

But she doesn't even wait until I respond. She's already cutting across the road, waving to me as she goes. It's not like her to bail on smoothies, or bail on anything, really. I try not to read too much into it—she's hooking up with someone. It can be distracting, and I've definitely had my own set of distractions this past year.

I go to the Vons alone and pick up a lemon ginger juice, which makes me wince with every sip. Then I wander the aisles, looking for anything I can bring back to Odie.

It's too much of a risk to keep pilfering from the breakfast bar or trying to get an extra meal here or there from the inn's kitchen. I don't know how long he's staying, but even if it's just one or two more days, that's too much time to be sneaking food down to him. I've decided I'll just load up on whatever provisions make sense, then he can ration them as he needs.

There's a bunch of power bars in the cereal aisle, so I grab those, and a box of Cheerios too. I fill the basket with some bottled water, like I promised him. Then I pick out some random things that seem useful. They have a flashlight and batteries that are pretty cheap, and I remind myself to get my old camping lantern from the back of my closet. It's probably not a bad idea to get the sleeping bag and camping chairs down too. My parents and I used to go camping on the northern tip of the island, up at Parsons Landing. But that was before my mom got sick, before everything changed and stress was the new normal for my dad. Sometimes it feels like he's carrying the weight of the world, holding it all on his shoulders.

Before long I've added some canned fruit and an extra can opener, and then a whole bunch of chips and three huge bags of trail mix. I'm checking out when I see Lenora, the chef at the Ogygia Inn, in the next line over. I keep my head down, trying to avoid eye contact, but as soon as she has her bag she comes over.

"What are you doing here?" she asks, looking at the last of the trail mix, which the freshman bag boy, Ben, is loading into a paper shopping bag. "I thought you and your dad swore off grocery shopping."

"Oh . . . hey . . ." I say. Lenora was best friends with my mom. Whenever we cook together, or I'm sous cheffing for her in the kitchen, she tells me stories about them working on a dive boat in their twenties, and all the trouble they'd get in. "I'm . . . going on a camping trip."

"Really? This weekend?"

She seems surprised. She has one of those cute rope reusable bags, like a chef out of a magazine. All she's bought is a bunch of onions and garlic.

"No . . . um . . . later in the summer," I lie. Thankfully,

Ben has done quick work with my grocery bags. They are officially packed, and I scoop them up, calling to her as I go. "I have to drop these off with a friend. I'll catch up with you later!"

When I get out of the store, I take a right instead of a left, going the opposite way from the inn. The last thing I want is to get stuck walking out with her, and then get roped into getting a ride with her in her golf cart. Then I'd have to elaborate on the fake camping trip that I'm going on . . . later in the summer? Why would I be buying groceries for a camping trip that's weeks away? And why would I be dropping those groceries off with my friend?

Make it make sense, Callie.

I'm getting farther into town, into the most touristy stretch of Catalina, where the sidewalks are thick with people strolling leisurely, checking their phones every now and then to see what restaurant or shop they're being routed to. There's a whole line of people waiting to get into the Lobster Trap, one of the most popular restaurants in town. I turn onto Crescent Avenue to take the long way back to the inn. Beside me, beyond the narrow strip of beach filled with picnickers and sunbathers, is the harbor. The pier juts out, all the boats anchored in perfectly symmetrical arcs running across the water. Two huge cruise ships are parked in the distance. Everything is red, white, and blue, in preparation for July Fourth. Little American flags are hung at every shop door; colorful banners say HAPPY 4TH!! and CELEBRATE!!

I turn back and see the casino, which isn't actually a casino and is continually confusing every tourist who comes through. It's this circular theater and ballroom with all this amazing architecture. It was built in the twenties. Now it holds the island's annual jazz festival. I'm nearing the end of Crescent Avenue, where I catch a glimpse of Lenora zipping around the corner in her golf cart, disappearing as she continues down Pebbly Beach Road, back toward the inn. I'm watching her go when I hear some boys laughing. A few yards out, I spot Brett and a few of his friends in the water. They have different floats. Brett keeps diving under, then tossing the girls off the inflatable watermelon slice and into the ocean.

Maybe it's what happened last night—this great reminder that I am strong and capable. Or maybe it's just the sight of him seeming so smug. He keeps going after this one girl in a navy string bikini, tossing her into the air. Something compels me—it's like before I even think, I'm moving, dropping my bags on the sand.

I go down the beach, to the blankets spread out near the shore. It takes me two seconds to find his teal hat—I recognize the rips and fading from the other night. It's in a pile of stuff: T-shirt, keys, and iPhone. I pick up the phone and stare at the wallpaper. It's of him and a girl with curly black hair in a tux and prom dress.

He has a girlfriend.

Of course he does.

"Hey!" I yell, holding the iPhone in the air. "This yours?"

The group turns, squinting into the sun. It takes a beat for Brett to register me—who I am and why I'm there. He's the first to start walking through the shallows, trying to get to me before I can do anything with his stuff. But I bring my arm back and throw the phone as far as I can. It makes a satisfying *thunk* as it disappears into the sea.

"You bitch!" he yells, so loud even the girl beside him flinches.

"That's right," I say, and smile. I way prefer *bitch* to *slut*.

Then I turn, strolling up the beach, and grab my bags. When I finally glance back, he is diving into the water, again and again, dredging the bottom for his phone.

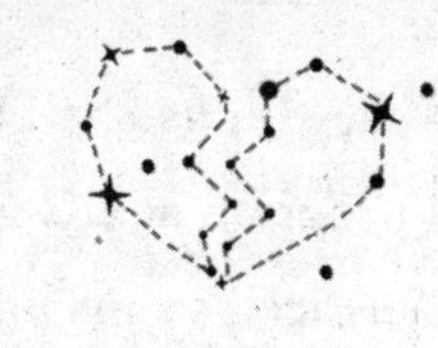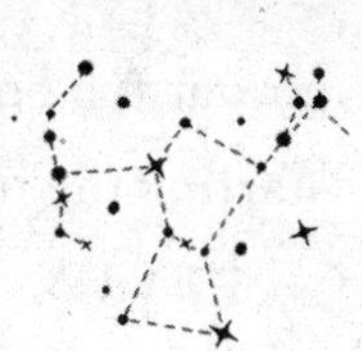

TEN

THE FIRST WEEK WITH ODIE

The dinner shift drags on and on, mainly because a solo writing retreat lady has camped out at the table in the corner. She keeps leisurely going back and forth between her roast chicken and her laptop. Sometimes she hums and sometimes she just stares out at the ocean, then smiles to herself, like she's just come up with the most brilliant idea.

"I don't think I can watch much more of this." Araceli, our server, leans on the lobby desk conspiratorially. "Every time I go to remove the plate she tells me she's not done. It's all bone and gristle at this point!"

"Why don't you just go home?" I say. "I can close her out and bus the table."

"You sure?"

"I'm going to lock everything up early tonight anyway. It's Sofia Alvarez's birthday party and my dad's letting me go out for once . . . he thinks she's a good influence. She's starting the premed program at UCLA."

"UCLA. Wow." Araceli seems impressed.

"I know."

"You might be here later than you think . . ." she says.

I wave her off. Araceli has a ten-year-old daughter at home—she doesn't need this. She squeezes my hand before telling the woman I'm taking over.

The rest of the lobby is quiet. It still has the same decor we've had since I was a kid. Large, comfy rattan chairs and sofas. Wood floors and high ceilings. Everything is a shade of white, gray, or pale blue, like you're in someone's beach house. The real draw has always been the view, and the giant windows that overlook the ocean. From the front desk I can see half the dining room, and I let Writing Retreat sit there on her laptop for a little bit longer. Then I disappear into the kitchen and reappear with a stuffed cupcake in a neat take-out box, giving it to her "for the road."

It's the not-so-subtle hint she needed.

After I lock up I stop at the apartment, checking to make sure my dad's already asleep. It's only nine o'clock but he's on the early shift tomorrow—starting at six—so I can trust he's out for the night. I drag the squashed grocery bag out from under my bed, along with the pack of bottled water, tucking each under an arm.

When I get to room 2 I knock, waiting for Odie to answer.

"It's just me," I say, and he finally comes to the door.

"Was that a test?" he asks. "Trying to see if I can follow directions?"

"Congratulations. You passed."

The room is so dark it takes my eyes a while to adjust. It's only then that I can see his silhouette, just barely visible against the glow of the side window. I didn't mean to do it, but I'm standing only a foot away from him, my face staring into his chest. I'm grateful he at least has a shirt on this time.

"What do I win?" he asks, leaning down.

"Respect. Just a little."

He's so close it startles me. I duck past him, putting the supplies onto the small table in the corner. I fumble for the flashlight, realizing too late that I bought the wrong batteries.

"Thank you for all this. For everything," he says.

"I bet you're dying of thirst."

"Not dying . . . but close."

He unscrews one of the water bottles and downs it in a few big gulps. Then he immediately opens another.

"I'm supposed to be somewhere tonight," I say. "I can bring by more supplies in the morning. I have some camping stuff I have to dig out of my closet."

"Oh."

It's hard to even see his expression, but I can hear the disappointment in his voice.

"Is the blanket terrible?" I ask.

"No, I just thought maybe we'd hang out."

I try to think through what that even means . . . does he actually want to hang out, or does he already have Stockholm syndrome? Now that I'm down here, dropping off food and water, it does feel a little bit like he's my captive. Wasn't I the one who said he couldn't talk to anyone or let anyone in the room?

"Look," I say. "You don't have to stay in here if you don't want. Just don't . . . don't tell anyone this is where you've been sleeping, okay? You have to be super careful about anyone seeing you coming or going. My dad cannot find out."

"No. Of course," he says. "I won't."

"You could walk into town tomorrow. Do you have clean clothes? Do you need any?"

"I have enough," he says. "Don't worry about me. I didn't mean to . . . you don't have to . . ."

He trails off, letting the words just hang there. It's like we're two voices, calling out to each other in the dark. I can see him shift on his feet, then turn slightly. But I still can't see his face.

It feels like something's shifting, though I can't tell what.

I'm already too involved. I'm really trying not to get in any deeper. . . .

"I'll check on you tomorrow," I say, and slip back out the door. "I'll bring the right batteries. And some other stuff for you. Promise."

He's still standing there, backlit by the window, when I pull the door shut behind me.

By the time I get to Sofia's party, all the birria is gone. Her mom and grandmother spent the days leading up to it marinading the meat and slow cooking it, but it was devoured in under an hour. I feast instead on the homemade tortillas, loading them up with carnitas and different salsas. The carnitas are a pretty great consolation prize.

"You're here," Pita says when she spots me by the door. "I didn't think you'd come."

"Why?"

I take a massive bite of my taco.

"Just 'cause . . ."

She folds her arms over her chest, a Topo Chico in one hand. Then she just shrugs.

"How'd it go with Zeke? Did you meet up with him before?"

Just asking about him is enough to break the tension between us. Pita's face gets all pink and flushed, and she tousles her hair with one hand. I wonder if I'm already too late to catch up—if something monumental already happened.

"We spent the whole day together," she says, leaning into me so no one else will hear. "He's cool. And we were basically naked together."

"Yes. I love this for you."

Two of Sofia's aunts walk into the living room, and Pita and I straighten, pretending we aren't talking about her hooking up with a guy she just met.

"It was really nice. He leaves soon, though."

"That's rough."

"He's going to Stanford, though, so maybe I'll see him up north."

"Wow . . . he's smart too."

"Yo! Callie!" a voice calls from across the room. "Where you been?"

Damian Brooks is headed toward me. He's six three, but I always think of him as being shorter, since he only shot up last year. He's wearing his UCSB sweatshirt—he's headed there in less than two months.

"I've been around," I say.

"Bullshit."

He sits on the back of Sofia's mom's couch, but one of Sofia's aunts gives him a dirty look. He climbs off and leans against the wall instead, where he's dangerously close to knocking over a whole bunch of family photos.

"I've been working, mainly." I look to Pita as I say it, like she can confirm. "Taking a lot of shifts. And then hanging with Pita."

"Does your dad pay you?" he asks. "He better be paying you. It's, like, illegal not to."

"Damian . . ." Pita rolls her eyes.

"What?"

"Of course he pays me," I say. "And I'm basically intern-ing with Lenora, our chef. I've been doing a lot of desserts there."

"When do you leave?" he asks, turning to Pita.

"August fifteenth," she says.

"Did you get your roommate assignment yet?" he asks.

Before she can answer, Danny Ramirez literally dives into the conversation, slinging his arm around Damian's neck. "I got mine yesterday. Some kid from Idaho. What am I going to do with some nerd from Idaho? What are we going to have in common?"

"Watch, he's going to be your best friend," Damian laughs. "You're going to be going home with him to Idaho and shit, telling everyone how much you love Idaho."

"For the record, Yellowstone is in Idaho. And other cool stuff," Pita adds.

Danny insists he's going to come home every break, at least in the beginning, because Catalina is the perfect place to come back to. Then they start getting into what they bought for their dorms so far, and if Pita's shipping stuff or she's just going to have her parents drive it all up when she moves in. Her family is making a big trip out of it—even her brothers are going to go to see her off. They discuss the meals at the dining halls, and how the school Danny is going to has fast-food restaurants in their food court. My thoughts drift to Odie and room 2 . . . how he had wanted me to stay with him, how I chose to come here tonight instead. . . .

I go to the bathroom, but then when I get out I just head for the door.

"Where you going?" Danny calls after me.

"I've got an early shift tomorrow," I say, which is a lie.

My friends don't question it, and even though I want Pita to come with me, she just stands there. Doesn't even make a move to leave. So I say goodbye to Sofia and her parents, and congratulate her and everything, and then I'm out.

As soon as I'm alone, walking on the cool, dark street, I realize something. I don't feel weird about going home early from a party with all my closest friends. I don't care that I just left and my best friend stayed, that she didn't even want to come with me.

Because going home now means something different. It's going back to a mystery that hasn't yet been revealed. To something exciting . . . and weird and wonderful. . . .

I'm going back to Odie.

ELEVEN

THE FIRST WEEK WITH ODIE

I'm in my own bed, surrounded by the quiet rush of the ocean. I didn't get back until really late, and technically I'm supposed to see Odie tomorrow, but I can't stop thinking about him . . . so much that it's impossible to sleep. I remember how close we were in the hotel room, how I didn't even realize he was there until he was just inches away. Or his voice—all raspy and cute when he asked if we were going to hang out.

I roll over and grab my phone off my nightstand. I haven't looked in a minute, but I do all my usual searches: *boy, Odie, missing, sailboat, Bieker Moth.* I search *Catalina* and *Odie,* but nothing comes up. Is he a figment of my imagination? Did I somehow convince myself I saved someone in some strange delusion? How could a teen boy disappear in a sailing accident and no one realize he's gone?

It doesn't take long before I decide to just go down there, because I need to find out. I retrieve all the old camping stuff from the back of my closet and grab AAA batteries—the kind we actually need for the flashlight. There's a portable stove and mini propane tanks, and I bring those too, thinking they might be useful if he's staying for a while.

Do I want him to stay for a while?

I'm packing as though he's staying forever.

He at least needs the lantern, I tell myself. It's a necessity, as much as food and water. I maneuver all the supplies out the front door and cut across the parking lot, taking the stairs down the side of the inn. Before I'm even at the door it's open and he's coming toward me, taking the sleeping bag and stove from my hands.

"How'd you know I was here?" I ask. "I figured you'd be sleeping."

"The stairs make this creaking sound whenever anyone comes down them," he says. "I thought this late it was either you . . . or someone coming to murder me."

"What if it's both?" I shoot him a sinister stare.

"Saving my life . . . only to take my life," he says. "Really playing the long game."

"Always."

As soon as I'm inside we disappear again, the room so dark I can't go more than a few feet without bumping into something. I feel for the camping lantern and turn it on, surprised at how much light it gives off.

"You give me water, food, light," he says. "You're a god."

"I'm glad you noticed."

He rolls the sleeping bag out on the bed, then opens the first aid kit, picking through some of the bandages and gauze.

"I know I was supposed to see you tomorrow," I say. "I just couldn't sleep . . ."

"Neither could I."

He smiles, and my head feels light. Like it was a dangerous thing, coming down here.

"You're being so kind to me," he says. "And I barely know anything about you. Except that you're crazy brave. I don't know if I would've jumped into the ocean to save a stranger."

He looks at me, his mouth curling up into his right dimple. I can't help but smile back, and then I have to turn away, because why am I smiling at that? At him?

"What?" he asks. "I'm being serious."

"No, I know you are."

"So?"

"I don't know . . . sometimes I feel like I'm hallucinating. Are you even real? This cute boy who I saved from a storm. . . ."

"So you think I'm cute."

"That's your takeaway?"

Now he's really smiling. He does this silly little strut, acting all cocky, and then we're both laughing. He's wearing a dirty tank top and bathing suit—the same thing he was in this morning—but I can see glimpses of him from his normal life. He's the guy you want to be friends with . . . and hook up with. He's fun.

"It's okay, don't be embarrassed," he says.

"I'm not."

He's flipping through the bandages he's pulled from the first aid kit, unsure what to do with them. I can see the cut on his back through his shirt.

"Need some help?" I ask.

"If you could . . . yeah."

He turns so his back is to the light. I peel the tank top away, revealing a long, uneven cut. I'm relieved to see it's not very deep. I wipe it with an alcohol pad and cover it with gauze and bandages, making sure it holds.

"This is from the wreck?" I ask.

"I think I got clipped when it capsized."

"It could have been so much worse."

"I know."

"Tell me again why you weren't wearing your life vest?"

"I just took it off for a beat. And then it fell, and I lost it."

It's suicidal to go out on the ocean, in that boat, without wearing a life vest. I'm starting to wonder if it wasn't as much of an accident as he says. If something in him wanted to be wrecked, destroyed.

It's like he can sense where my mind is going.

He taps my arm, says, "Thanks for doing that."

He turns back around and sits on the edge of the bed. I sit on the chair in the corner, organizing the last of the items. I notice about half the food I brought before is already gone. I put the new batteries into the flashlight and switch it on, just to check that it works.

"This was all really nice of you. Getting me all this stuff," he says. "I found my wallet—it was tucked in one of the side pockets of my jacket. I might go into town tomorrow and see if my ATM card works. I might be able to pay you back."

"You're good."

"Seriously, though. This is so . . . kind."

"It's just the decent thing to do," I say. "You're in trouble. You need help. I don't even fully understand why, but I'm here so I'm helping."

Besides, the inn might be struggling—it's probably obvious even to Odie—but I'm not going to take money from someone who's stranded, far from home, and not sure what to do next. That just feels wrong.

"So . . . ? Will you tell me something about you? Anything?" he asks.

"Like what?"

I was fiddling with the corner of the stove, where the little Coleman logo is, but I stop to look at him. Mainly because he hasn't stopped looking at me.

"What's it like living here? It feels really separate from everything."

"It is really separate," I say. "There's good things and bad things about living on an island."

He doesn't say anything, just waits for me to go on.

"I love the winters," I say. "When it's mainly locals again. Like we get our island back. And I love going down to the beach every day, or just having the ocean be part of my life. It's what I wake up to every morning and what I go to bed to every night."

"But . . ."

"But it's an island. You can feel really trapped sometimes. Kind of . . . stuck."

"You're a senior, right?" he says. "You'll be gone soon anyway."

"Actually . . . no."

It's like we're speeding toward train tracks, and I don't know if we'll get snagged on them or not. This could be where things end. Is he going to judge me for not going to college? Think I'm some kind of loser, or dumb?

"You're not going to college?" He seems surprised. "Is it a money thing?"

"It's an everything thing," I say. "But no. I'm not going."

"You don't want to talk about it."

But then I find that I am . . . and I do. I tell him how I did okay in school and I had my list of colleges that I wanted to apply to. But then when it came time to do all the work, I kept getting sidetracked, and no matter how many times my dad reminded to get my applications together I never was able to finish. It just felt like this monumental task. I couldn't even get it together to revise the personal essays required for my applications. When I sent them in they were still kind of a mess. I only got into one school—my safety—and I didn't even want to go there. And then things got really weird for me at the end of the year, and I didn't feel good about making any decisions about anything . . . or moving away from Catalina.

"Where did you want to go?" he asks.

"If I'm being totally honest . . . I don't think a traditional college is for me. I'm more of a tactile person. I learn by doing. I have an unofficial internship with our chef at the inn, and I've been making a lot of the desserts. And then I kind of experiment and make my own stuff."

"Like what? How do you even know where to start?"

I smile, because no one's really asked me about my desserts before. Pita's eaten dozens of my stuffed cupcakes at this point, but it's more of a taste tester situation. She's never really been interested in the hows or whys behind each dessert. Even my dad, as encouraging as he tries to be, zones out when I start talking about different recipes I'm working on.

"I do these thick cookies that have different chocolate bars crushed into them. Butterfingers, Snickers, sometimes Reese's cups."

"Damn. And you have me eating canned fruit."

"I haven't had time to make a new batch of anything," I say, then I lower my voice, trying to sound all serious. "I've had more important matters to attend to."

"What else do you make?"

"Stuffed cupcakes, double-stuffed chocolate chunk bars—where I mix a bunch of candy ingredients together.

Trail mix chocolate bars. Basically desserts on top of desserts, mixed in with desserts. That's kind of my brand."

I don't know why I say "brand," like I'm some kind of influencer or something. I don't even post anything on my Instagram about it. It still feels like this secret life I'm leading, that I've only shared with friends and family. If I said it out loud—that maybe culinary school would be best for me, that that's the dream—I'd have to deal with the reality that it might not be possible.

"Wait . . . so . . ." He slips down to the floor, leaning his back against the bed. He's got his elbows propped up on his knees, and he's studying me. "What did you mean when you said things got weird at the end of the year? That you didn't want to make any big decisions . . ."

"It's complicated."

"Try me."

Where do I even start? How do I explain what happened between me and Harper Thorne, and why I even took that picture? Some of the guys at my school know about it, and they were all pretty sweet, saying they were going to find Harper and fight him. Defend my honor, et cetera, et cetera. But telling Odie? When he knows so little about me?

"It's not a good story," I say.

"I mean, you don't have to talk about it if you don't want to," he says. "But I have a lot of not-so-great stories too. I mean—that's why I'm here."

He has a point. He's living in an abandoned hotel room,

running away from his family. No one even knows he's here except me.

So I start at the beginning, saying how I met Harper over spring break and he love bombed me (a phrase I only learned recently), being crazy romantic and stuff as soon as we met. And then how we hooked up a bunch when he was on the island, and how he went cold on me after. And how I couldn't understand what had happened, and I started feeling like I did something wrong. And then the picture . . . and finding out he'd shared it . . .

"What a fucking asshole," Odie says. "Dickish dickhead. Whoa."

"Yeah . . . it seems that way."

"I'm so sorry, Callie," he says, and his brown eyes are huge and glossy. "You didn't deserve that. I'm just so sorry."

"It's fine," I say. "It's only my boobs. One boob, really— you couldn't see the other one."

"It's not fine. It is definitely not fine. You could sue him."

"His dad is this tech behemoth. Titan of industry and all that. They'd bury us."

He pops up from the floor and comes over to me, sitting on the chair on the other side of the table. He leans in, and the lantern light warms his skin.

"I want to punch him in the face," he says. "And I've never even punched anyone in the face. I really consider myself a pacifist."

"Thanks," I say. "For being cool about it."

"There's nothing to be cool about . . . you didn't do any-thing wrong," he says. "It's just a double standard for guys and girls. A guy hooks up with a dozen girls and he's a 'player' or a 'ladies' man.' But it always has this connotation that he's really cool. But if a girl does it she's a slut. What is this, the nineties? Like . . . when are we going to get past this stuff?"

"You sound really progressive," I say.

"I guess it was my parents' divorce. Watching them get back out there after . . . it was really hard for my mom. Like, I almost can't blame her that she's with my stepdad. He at least has a job. Some of the guys she went out with were such bottom-feeders."

"Now I'm convinced I really am hallucinating you."

"It's a mutual hallucination," he says, leaning in. "But then . . . you seem like the realest person I've ever met."

He doesn't look away. There's a softness in his expression now, the lantern light reflected in his eyes. It seems for a moment he might come closer, move in for a kiss. But instead we stay like that, staring at each other, until I look away.

"I should probably get back . . ." I say, standing.

My whole body feels flushed. I'm in this hotel room, alone, with this boy who feels like magic. Everything about him is perfect—almost too good to be true. The old me would be thrilled, hopeful, but right now I'm worried. What if I'm making a mistake? What if he's not who he says he is? What if the same thing just happens all over again?

I don't know anything about Odie.

He's still a stranger to me.

"Yeah, of course," he says, and again there's that tinge of disappointment in his voice.

He walks me to the door, and it's like I can feel every movement of his body behind me, hear every step. Am I really going to leave him here right now? Am I really going back to my bed, to sleep alone?

I have to. I shouldn't get involved . . . not in that way.

You have to protect yourself, my father said after he found out what had happened with Harper Thorne. *These guys come to this island and think they can do whatever they want. You have to be careful.*

Is Odie just another one of those guys?

It's like he can sense what I'm thinking. He slows his steps, gives me more space. When I finally turn to look at him, his expression is serious and removed.

"Thank you again for helping me," he says. "I went out before and I looked at the boat. I think if I can just get a tool kit or something, I could probably have it fixed within a day or two. I'll stitch the sail. I can get moving, maybe sail back."

"I don't think that's a good idea. It's so far. . . ."

"Otherwise I'll have to get it towed. It'll be a whole thing. This time I'll wear a life jacket, I swear. I'll go in the middle of the day."

Now that it feels more real, I immediately don't want him to leave. It's too soon.

"I guess I can get you a tool kit. We have one somewhere."

"I'll wait for perfect weather."

"I still think the ferry would be safer," I offer, but I'm already mad at myself for saying it. Why am I agreeing with him that he should leave?

Am I crazy, thinking things with Odie could be different?

That there's something here I've never felt before?

"Thank you again," he says. "I'm just grateful the stars aligned the other night. If it wasn't for you, I don't know what would've happened."

"I don't even want to think about it."

Then he does the hottest, most excruciating thing. He leans down and kisses me on the cheek, his lips just grazing the side of my face. As he does, his hand comes up to my chin and holds it in place.

It is delicate . . . and gentle.

And my whole body responds, every inch of my skin screaming out for more.

"Good night, Callie," he says.

"Good night," I repeat.

Then I take a step back, out the door, and he closes it gently.

It takes me a while to move from that spot, to drag myself up the stairs and back to my bed, where I curl up. Elated, buzzing from the feeling of his lips on my skin . . .

And completely alone.

TWELVE

THE FIRST WEEK WITH ODIE

"Are you sure you don't have another room available? Something with a view?" The woman looks at me over her glasses. "Can you check again?"

I've checked twice—the first time just to confirm we were booked, as I knew we were, and the second time just to appease her. I can't bring myself to check a third time, even as a performance. This lady is deranged.

"I wish I could help you," I say. "But it's high season. Every hotel on the island is booked. When you made your reservation, unfortunately you did request the garden room."

The garden room. That's what she's really pissed about. I told my dad not to label them like that, because it was inevitable that guests would show up and feel hoodwinked. That block of rooms looks out over the garden, yes, but also the small parking lot where employees park and we keep our two Ogygia Inn golf carts. It's almost offensive to walk into the hotel and see the vast expanse of ocean out the windows . . . and then realize you're going to spend your entire stay looking at asphalt.

She turns back to her husband, who's standing there sheepishly. Gives him a look like *Can you believe this?*

"It's fine, Rita," he whispers. "Come on."

But she's got her elbows on the lobby desk, and she keeps breathing heavy, like this garden room is really affecting her health. If I don't do something, she's going to be here all afternoon.

"You know what? I'd love to give you some complimentary lunch vouchers for tomorrow. Our chef, Lenora, is incredible. I know she's cooking up something delicious."

Rita tilts her head, then turns back to her husband, as if considering it. Instead of waiting for her to answer, I simply pull the vouchers from the drawer and set them in front of her. After a beat, she takes them, rolls her eyes, then walks off. I hear her muttering something about the golf carts under her breath.

As soon as she's gone, I feel my whole body unclench. I can't believe this is just life now, that soon there will be no school or friends as a respite. I'll just work here, at the inn, and help Lenora out when I can, and go to the beach. My dad only gave me a slight bump up from minimum wage, so I'm at twenty dollars an hour now. I have about twelve hundred dollars saved. It's not enough to get anywhere.

To move away from here, and all this.

It's strange; there was something about saying what I wanted out loud to Odie that changed things. It's as if my dreams are more potent now, after the other night. There's more friction between how things are and how I want things to be. I didn't let myself go down to see him yesterday or this morning. Instead I dropped off another case of water and some tools in front of room 2, careful not to make a sound on the steps as I went down.

It just feels like it's for the best. Like there's no point in thinking about this stuff if there's nothing I can actually do about it.

It'll be better if he fixes the boat and leaves.

Another guest comes over, asking for toothpaste. He's an elderly gentleman and he's forgotten his. I dig around in our supply stash, looking for one. We have extra razors and dental floss . . . some samples of face wash. When I finally retrieve the toothpaste and look up, I'm not sure what I'm seeing.

Walking into the lobby is Odie. Only it's not . . . It's like the real-life version of him. He has on a clean blue linen button-down shirt and a new navy bathing suit I don't recognize. He must've washed up in the ocean, because his hair is styled, the waves in it more pronounced as they fall over his forehead.

When he locks eyes with me, his whole face explodes in a smile and it's more than I can even stand. He is so unbelievably beautiful.

The older gentleman is there, waiting for his toothpaste.

He clears his throat to signal that he still exists. I slowly hand over the tiny box and stand up straighter as Odie strides over to the front desk. His face is all light—he looks so happy.

"Before you say anything, I'm sorry for coming up here. I know this is your work, and I don't want your dad to see me," he says. "But I needed to tell you something."

On instinct I look over my shoulder, to the office door. My dad is inside, figuring out where we're at with this month's budget, and I instinctively turn, blocking Odie from view. The last thing I need is him coming out here and seeing us talking.

"I worked on the boat all yesterday," he says. "And it's in decent shape. Better than decent—I was surprised that I was able to get so much of it fixed. But it's like . . . I keep trying to picture myself leaving and I can't. Not yet."

He's watching me closely, his eyes scanning my face. Part of me wants to smile, but I'm scared about where this is going. Why does he want to stay? Is this really about me, or is it about something else entirely? What is he running from?

"It might sound crazy, but I just think . . . I don't know. That there's more for me here."

"It doesn't sound crazy," I say.

"So I guess what I'm asking . . ."

His cheeks redden, the color coming through his tan. He runs his fingers along the front of the lobby desk. He's so nervous, I can't help but smile, and then he's smiling too.

"I guess I wanted to know if you'd go out with me to-night?" he finally says.

I turn to the office door again, to make sure my dad hasn't suddenly appeared. I'm scanning the faces of everyone in the lobby and the dining hall. It feels impossible that they'd all be going about their day, just eating or planning their snorkeling trip when this is happening to me. When Odie, did-I-imagine-him Odie, is asking me on a date.

"Yeah, of course, yes," I finally manage.

There's something about this that feels almost unbearably formal. If only because of the overhead lights, the buttoned shirt. The guests who pass through the lobby. Every now and then Matty looks over from his post at the door, trying to figure out who this guy is and why he's never seen him before.

It's strange to be in public with Odie. It feels like some kind of confirmation that he exists, that this is real. That everything about him isn't too good to be true.

"I'll meet you outside in a little bit?" he asks. "What time do you get off?"

"Six," I say. "But how would you even know? It's not like you have your phone."

"How about we meet at sunset."

"Romantic. I like it."

"I like us," he says. "Down at the beach?"

I nod. Then he backs away, watching me as he goes. It's not until he's left that I can tell I'm sweating—my shirt is sticking to my chest, my neck. I keep hearing his voice in my head, keep feeling his eyes on me . . .

"*Not yet.*"

He's right—he can't go.

Something has already opened up inside me, and I don't think I can pretend I'm the same person I was before. There's still too much unfinished between us, too much unsaid.

There are things I still need to find out.

We go to a restaurant on the other side of town, where I'm certain my dad, and Pita's parents, won't see us. It's one of my favorites but I haven't been in over a decade, since before my mom died. They have this thick focaccia bread that has the perfect amount of oil and rosemary on it, the salt flakes so big they look like sugar on top. I ordered the penne alla vodka and nearly started frothing at the mouth when they plopped it down in front of me.

"This is incredible," Odie says between bites.

He's eating twice as fast as me, and he's already finished his tortellini. Now he's ripping the bread into tiny pieces and dragging it along the edge of the bowl, trying to get every last bite. I feel like maybe I've been starving him.

"Should I get you more food?" I ask. "The trail mix not doing it?"

He laughs. "Is it that bad? My mom says I eat like a Tasmanian devil."

"I just feel bad. You've been locked away for a few days with canned fruit."

"You have nothing to feel bad about." Then he looks at me and raises his eyebrows. "Besides, I got out a little."

He already told me all about his first adventure in town, where he managed to use the ATM, then proceeded to go to one of the boutiques and buy, essentially, a bunch of resort wear. Now he looks like he's on permanent vacation. He even has a sweatshirt that has CATALINA ISLAND in big white embroidered letters.

"How come you never told me Catalina Island is known as the island of romance?" he asks as the waiter takes away our plates.

"Would've been weird if I did," I say. "Hey, Guy I Don't Know Well, do you know this island you wrecked on is known as the island of *romance*? What do you think of that?"

I give him a fake sexy stare, batting my eyelashes.

"See, I would've liked that. You totally misread me."

"I was too worried about you. I wasn't exactly trying to flirt."

"I know . . ."

He's quiet, and when the waiter drops the check he immediately goes for it, even though I reach for my purse. He pulls a hundred-dollar bill off a thick wad from his wallet. Then he sets it on the tray.

"Okay, now I'm freaked out," I say. "Are you a bank robber?"

"Bank robbers aren't really a thing anymore. It's more like crypto thieves and hackers and fraudsters and stuff."

"So you're one of those," I say.

"You're so skeptical of me. I like it." He laughs. "But no.

I transferred all my bar mitzvah money into a bank account before I left. It wasn't an official plan or anything . . . but I wasn't sure if I'd actually go back."

"Wait . . . bar mitzvah?"

Did I hear that correctly?

"What?"

"I just thought your parents were Mexican American . . . Is that a dumb white-person thing to say? You're Jewish?"

"My mom is Jewish, so I was bar mitzvahed and everything. My dad is Mexican American—his parents were from Oaxaca. I don't think it's a dumb white-person thing to say? I mean, I do look just like my dad. . . . What are you?"

"Italian, Irish, a little Welsh. But my great-grandmother was actually Mexican too—from Chihuahua."

"Ahhhhh . . ." He raises his brows again.

When we leave he pulls back my chair in this super polite way, like we're a couple in a romantic comedy. It's so formal I almost think he's joking. But it's there, obvious in everything he does—he comes from a different world. A world of Tiffany's table manners and crystal vases, void of past due notices and wrinkled T-shirts.

This is the last person I should be getting involved with.

We take the back road out of the restaurant, away from Crescent Avenue, where the tourist crowds thin out and there are only a few shops and restaurants open past sunset. I told my dad I was going to Pita's house and crossed my fingers that the inn was busy enough tonight that he never bothered checking in. I texted Pita to warn her she was my cover—but she's been so busy anyway, she'd never randomly stop by. She's spending every last second with Zeke. I got a text this morning with the pointing hand sign repeated five times, then the meme'd pinch sign.

I'm still not even totally sure what she meant.

"You're serious about not going back, like officially running away?" I say when we turn up the road. "I think your parents will be pretty pissed. And I don't know how far you could even get on bar mitzvah money."

"You'd be surprised," he says.

"Seriously, though."

"No, I know it's not a real option. I just had to get away for a while."

"Your stepdad is that bad? Aren't you going to college next year?"

"I'm not sure . . . that's part of the fight. My dad is insisting I go to his alma mater—it's like that's the only way I'll have any kind of future. But I've always wanted to stay in Los Angeles. The East Coast isn't for me."

I don't ask what the alma mater is, because I'm sure it'll be some fancy Ivy League school I could never have gotten into. And even if I did get in, we never could have afforded it. It can't just be about school, though, or family. There's something else.

His dad is a narcissist—not a serial killer.

"I don't think I'd like the East Coast either . . . I couldn't survive in the cold," I say.

"Seasons are overrated."

"Truth."

The back of our hands brush against each other, and I want him to just grab mine, to hold it. Every second he doesn't makes me want it more. It's distracting, and I'm suddenly conscious of all the space between his body and mine. I can hear every step we take against the pavement and his breaths, mingling with the sounds of the ocean.

"Now that I'm here, though . . ." he says, slowing down. "Maybe this is where I should be. Ocean in every direction, sailing."

"Catalina Island," I say. "You're serious."

"It's really peaceful. And you're here too. . . ."

I stop walking before he does. It's hard to even look at him; it's all too familiar, too obvious.

"Don't do that," I say. "Do not be another cocky guy, waltzing in here for the summer, making promises you can't keep. I've heard it all before—trust me."

"I'm not," he says, holding up his hands.

"So you're going to live on Catalina Island." I'm almost laughing as I say it. "You're going to . . . what? Stay in our decrepit room for the rest of your life, bathing and pooping in the ocean? Get a job at the ice cream store for eighteen dollars an hour?"

"Maybe I'd just stay for a couple months. I don't know—I haven't really thought it all through."

"Yeah, that much is clear."

He shrugs, like *I'm just throwing out ideas.* He doesn't understand how dangerous those ideas are for me . . . how enticing. Of course I want him to stay. I want to believe that this could actually be something. But it's going to end the way all these things end—with him sailing away and me staying, heartbroken, in a place that now reminds me of him.

I can't do this again.

"This isn't supposed to be happening—" I say. "I was never meant to get involved with you. It's only going to be bad for me."

"No . . ."

"Yes, Odie. Yes."

"Listen to me," he says, and he has both my hands now. We're standing in someone's driveway, next to two motorbikes. He takes a step, then pulls me farther down it. The souvenir shop on the other side of us is closed. "I don't have anything figured out right now but I don't need to. I really like you, Callie. And if you don't like me then you can just say that . . . but I don't think that's true."

"I do, but . . ."

"No buts, then," he says, and he's smiling now, holding my hands together in front of his heart. "It would be dumb not to try for something. It would be a waste. We don't have to know everything right now."

He's leaning into me, our lips getting closer, and I know as soon as he kisses me that that's it—it's over. I will never want to stop.

I've only made it this far because we've barely even touched.

"We'll take it in moments," he says. "Don't you want to?"

I can smell the soap on his skin, the boutique smell still in his shirt. He's studying me with those brown eyes, searching my expression for some kind of sign that I want this—that I want *him*. Any chance of resisting him is over.

It feels like everything I've known is over. . . .

I launch into him, our lips meeting, and the taste of him is almost too much. With every kiss I want more, our mouths kneading against each other. He drops my hands and brings his palms to my cheeks, cradling my face in his, his chin hard against mine.

We slam against the wall, and every inch of my body is on alert. It's somehow everything and not enough, and I'm already craving more. I bury my fingers in his hair, kissing him deeper, until we eventually break apart to breathe.

He looks at me, stunned, and smiles. Then he rests his forehead against mine.

"We'll take it in moments," I repeat.

He lands one last kiss on my lips, my cheek.

"In moments . . ." he says.

THIRTEEN

THE SECOND WEEK WITH ODIE

The texts from Pita sit, unanswered, in my phone. I keep going back to them, thinking through how to respond.

We've always spent July Fourth together. There's a huge golf cart parade in town that everyone goes crazy for, then a dinghy parade out on the water. A bunch of bands play on Wrigley Stage and the streets turn into a massive party, all the tourists mixing with locals. I can't remember a year Pita and I didn't sit on the rock wall at Descanso Beach, watching the fireworks explode over the bay. But here she is, texting me like I'm a stranger, asking what I'm doing.

"Phone," my dad calls from over my shoulder.

"I'm off in two minutes," I say.

"It sets a bad example," he says, walking over so he's beside me, behind the lobby desk. He smooths his hands over the top of it. The front is made out of different pieces of driftwood, assembled in an artful cascade to give the place a cozy beach feel. He smiles at an older woman in a caftan as she passes. "No one else looks at their phone at work, and I don't want guests wondering about Wi-Fi."

"No one even saw," I say as I put it back under the desk.

"Not the point."

He busies himself with the computer. He's entering a cancellation for next week—so it makes sense why he's so stressed. It's been such a fight to keep the inn afloat, and a last-minute cancellation is lost money. It's unlikely anyone would book just a few days out.

I want to tell him not to worry, that it's okay, but I don't know that it is anymore. Only he has access to the inn's budget and financial information. It's not like he doesn't have options, though—I've fielded the calls from real estate developers. It feels like every other month one reaches out, putting in a formal inquiry about whether he has any interest selling. The place is in the perfect position—far enough away from town that it feels secluded but close enough that guests can still walk there. It's the only hotel that was built on this side of the island, before building codes changed. I know he feels loyalty to our family and he doesn't want to sell . . . but I worry if he keeps waiting the situation will get so dire it won't be his choice anymore.

"Texting Pita?" he asks.

"It is Fourth of July . . . we usually do something," I say, because that, at least, is the truth.

"I don't mind you going out with her," he says. "I know it's tradition. Just come back before ten. All the drunks come out after the fireworks. It's like the night of the living dead."

"I will. Promise."

My shift ends and I grab my phone and head off, but my dad doesn't even look up from the computer. It's definitely easier this way—I don't have to say anything more about Pita or answer any questions about my plans—but it still feels crappy. It's like he's always in his own world, preoccupied with other things.

Here, but not really.

When I get into the apartment I run the shower and start getting ready. I open up my texts again and draft one to Pita, then delete it. I try something else, then delete that too. The reality is, she's already decided to ditch me and hang out with Zeke. There's no way I'm going to tag along as their third wheel—it's beyond awkward. I don't need a pity invite.

And even if she doesn't know it, I made a decision too. I told Odie we could hang out tonight, that I would come get him when I was off work. It's not like we're going to have a double date with Pita and Zeke. I still have to keep every-thing with Odie secret—or as secret as it can be, considering.

I finally settle on something vague.

CALLIE

NM

COOL, SEE U DOWN THERE

The bathroom is already steamy, the mirror and shower door fogged up. I watch as the little ellipses on Pita's text appear and then disappear. Then they start up again. I wait, thinking she might push and say she wants me to come with them. But then the ellipses stop.

Pita doesn't write back, so I tell myself I don't care.

It doesn't matter, I think, then step into the wall of hot water.

"It almost feels like we're normal," Odie says, and he nudges my arm with his, leaning into me. He insisted on buying us two towering ice cream cones—mine strawberry and choco-late, and his three heaping piles of mint.

"Speak for yourself—I was always normal," I say.

A river of strawberry cream dribbles down my wrist. I lean forward, licking it to stop the flood. As soon as I do, Odie throws his head back and groans.

"What are you even doing to me right now?"

"*Ohhh . . .*" I say, all pretend sexy. "*You like this?*"

He leans over so his lips are inches from my ear. "I like everything about you. Just stop pretending like you're normal."

"Fine," I say, and the street is so packed with tourists I take my chance and kiss him once, hard, on the lips. The mint taste is sharp and sweet.

"I just meant this feels like where I should be," he says, "and what I should be doing. It's like we're a real couple."

"I don't think we can be a real anything until you tell me your last name."

"Fair," he says, cocking his head. He runs a hand through his hair. "If it means anything, I just don't want it to cloud your view of me."

"Let me guess, your mom is a famous singer."

"No." He shakes his head.

"Your dad," I say. "They were some fancy LA celebrity power couple and you've spent your whole life being used by people who just want to know them. It's been horrible for you, growing up like that, constantly in their shadow."

"No . . ." he says, and lets out a low laugh. "It's just simpler this way. Trust me?"

But I feel like I hit on something . . . like maybe I came close?

"I wouldn't tell them you're here. If that's what this is about."

"I don't think that. It's just . . . complicated."

"Isn't everything?"

Nearly every store and restaurant we pass has a Fourth of July display in the window. Red, white, and blue streamers are wrapped around every lamppost and handrail. Half the people in the crowd are wearing some version of the flag, whether it be shirts with stars or red and white stripes. I went with a cherry-red sundress I got at a thrift store last fall, with thin straps and ruching at the waist. Walking alongside Odie, I feel like myself.

Or really—a confident, more sophisticated version of myself.

We're just off Crescent Avenue, and as we approach the corner I catch sight of Pita and Zeke, his arm around her shoulder as they walk up toward the casino and Descanso Beach Club. Half our high school watches the fireworks from there, so I wasn't going to take Odie that way anyway, but now that I've spotted Pita I feel weird.

"What is it?" he asks.

He finishes the last of his ice cream cone and tosses the little paper holder and crumpled napkins in the trash. He's looking where I'm looking, trying to figure out why I stopped walking. The crowd parts around us.

"I just saw someone I know."

"You don't have to keep me hidden anymore," he says. "Eventually we will run into someone you're friends with."

"My dad would not be psyched about me dating someone right now," I say.

"Well, was that your dad?"

"No, he's at the hotel. But still . . ."

He raises his eyebrows at me, as if that proves his point. Then he slings his arms around my waist and pulls me into him, our hips touching. It's the closest I've been to him since we made out last night. He tucks a strand of my hair behind my ear and then leans down, so he's looking right at me.

"I'm here and I'm staying. At some point you're going to have to get used to me. Everyone will."

"Wow . . . you've really committed to this whole 'I'm staying on Catalina forever' thing."

"I'm staying as long as humanly possible, is that better?" he says.

"Now I kind of prefer the *forever* part," I say.

He kisses me again, so gently it stings my eyes. Everything he does has this sweetness to it, like this is different— something I can trust. I don't want to believe him but I do.

"Maybe tonight you can still be just mine, though," I whisper. "It can still be just us."

"I like the sound of that."

I wrap my arms around his neck and let myself fall into him, enjoying the warmth of his mouth, the way his breath flutters against my cheek whenever we pause for even a moment. I'm so lost in it—in him—I'm not sure what's happening when someone bumps me hard in the back.

"What the hell?" I say, turning to look. "Excuse you."

A few boys are already past us, walking toward the main drag with Solo cups in their hands. One of them walked into me, almost as if on purpose, and I can't tell if he's just super drunk or what. It was enough to knock me off-balance. I'm about to turn back to Odie when one guy spins around, nodding at me.

"You thought you'd get away with that?" he calls out.

It's Brett.

"What is he talking about?" Odie asks me.

"Tell him how you stole my phone," Brett yells. He's walking toward us now. The two guys he's with seem conflicted. One is looking around, embarrassed, while the other seems equally pissed. It seems like they've been drinking for a while . . . maybe all afternoon. "She stole my phone and threw it in the ocean."

"Way to simplify the story," I say. "Just walk away."

"Fuck off. Don't tell me what to do," Brett spits.

"You know him?" Odie looks utterly confused. He steps to the side, positioning himself so he's just a little in front of me.

"No—not really," I say, but I can feel my face getting hot. This is the absolute worst time for this. Shouldn't Brett be off the island by now? Slinking back to whatever cave he crawled out of?

"I said two words to him," I say.

"Oh, I heard all about your family's crappy inn," he says. "How it's falling apart and only people who can't get rooms anywhere else stay there."

I don't want to get into it with him, but it's hard to

listen to. It's like my body is having a physical reaction to every word.

"You don't know anything about me," I say.

Then he steps around Odie, so fast I don't even realize what's happening. He throws the beer he's holding onto my dress. My beautiful red dress. It splashes up on my face, covers part of my hair, and drips down my arm. I wish I could sink into the sidewalk, just let it swallow me up.

"I know a white trash whore when I see one," he says.

Then he walks away, back toward the ocean. Odie follows, and I want to call out for him to stop and just let it go, but it feels like a hand is closing around my throat. I can barely breathe and my eyes are hot. It takes everything I have not to cry.

"Hey!" Odie calls.

But Brett is already deeper into the crowd, weaving down to the beach. Odie speeds up and taps him on the shoulder. As soon as he turns around, Odie punches him hard in the stomach. Brett doubles over, the wind knocked out of him.

Odie clutches his fist as he runs back to me, his eyes wide with shock. When he's close, he grabs my arm and pulls me along with him.

"Come on," he says.

He's practically sprinting now, and I'm just trying to keep up.

FOURTEEN

We run, waiting to hear the sound of pattering feet behind us. I lead Odie up Tremont Street and then cut over, back down to Crescent, where I know the crowds will be thicker. It's getting late and everyone is moving toward the bay to see the fireworks. Blankets slung over their shoulders, folded beach chairs tucked under their arms. People are already cheering and yelling to each other and we move against the current— the only ones walking in the opposite direction.

When I finally glance back, Brett and his friends are gone. I wasn't sure if they followed us to begin with, but I wouldn't put it past Brett to come out of nowhere and tackle Odie to the pavement. Land a few brutal, retaliatory blows. He just seems like that kind of guy.

Odie keeps shaking out his right hand. He wraps his other hand around it, then squeezes it tight, kneading his knuckles.

"I've never done that before," he says, glancing over his

shoulder. "I've never hit anyone before. I swear."

He doesn't seem like the type to hit someone, or jump into a fight for fun, but it's a reminder that we only just met a week ago. I don't actually know what type of person he is. But he seems almost embarrassed now, like it was a moral failing or something.

"I believe you," I say.

And I realize I do.

Besides, there was something vaguely satisfying about watching Odie hit Brett. Don't get me wrong—I don't think it's right to hurt anyone, no matter what the circumstances are. I don't stomp ants or spiders, and for as long as I can remember my parents and I would carry insects and lizards out of the inn in glasses, sliding a piece of paper over the top to be extra safe. But what were we supposed to do? Just stand there, letting him hurl the most vile insults? How far would he have taken it?

"Really," Odie says. "I don't know . . . he was just being such an asshole."

"You should have seen him the other night. I'm not sure what was worse."

He takes two quick steps to catch up to me. Then he leans down, studying my expression. "Did he do something to you? What happened?"

"No, he didn't do anything to me," I say. "It was just more of the same. It's like Hawthorne Winfield just cranks out these entitled, rotten kids. Like that's a prerequisite for going there."

Odie narrows his eyes. He turns around, glancing at the

street behind us. The crowds have thinned out. It feels like we're alone now.

"He goes to Hawthorne Winfield? Seriously?" he asks.

"Uh-oh . . . why? Do you go to Hawthorne Winfield?"

"No . . ." he says. "I just . . ."

"What?"

I can tell there's something behind his words—I'm just not sure how bad it is or how nervous to be. Is he friends with Hawthorne Winfield kids? How would he even know them?

"I'm from LA," he says. "A lot of the private school circles overlap."

"You think he knows who you are?"

"I hope not. . . ." He kicks at the pavement with his toe. "I don't know, though."

"Where in Los Angeles are you from?" I ask.

It seems like a simple question, but it can reveal so much. I've been to LA enough times to know the difference between Highland Park and Brentwood, between Lincoln Heights and Beverly Hills. Each neighborhood has its own distinct vibe. Silver Lake and Los Feliz used to be for artists but they've each gentrified over the years, and now all the creative types have been pushed east (along with all the families the artists pushed out). Koreatown, Thai Town, and Little Armenia have retained their culture and their food scenes—I've had one of the best khao sois of my life in a little strip mall on Western.

You can also tell a lot about how much money someone has by what neighborhood they live in. I don't say that, though.

"Why do you ask?" He cocks a brow at me.

"Why are you avoiding the question?" I cock my brow too.

"If I told you, are you going to judge me?"

"Probably."

He laughs. "At least you're honest. My dad lives in Beverly Hills."

"Fancy."

I try to play it off, but *fancy* is an understatement. They make TV shows and movies about Beverly Hills because it's its own ecosystem of the one percent of the one percent. The cheapest houses are, like, fifteen million dollars. Beyoncé, Justin Bieber, Adele, Taylor Swift—they all live in Beverly Hills.

We walk in silence for a while, and eventually the inn's parking lot and main entrance are visible up ahead. We have a very dramatic, long, winding driveway that goes up the hill, high above all the shops and houses. At a certain point I just decide to bring it up—what do I have to lose?

"The boat," I say. "I knew because of the boat."

"You knew what?"

"That you weren't some sad, poor abused kid running away from home. That boat is, what? Forty thousand dollars? More?"

I already feel gross, mentioning money, but it's just the truth. Odie and I are from different worlds—it's apparent in the way we talk, in the way we dress. At dinner, he perched his finger on the back of his fork and it just screamed *rich kid*.

"I know it must seem like I'm some kind of spoiled brat, complaining about stupid things. I only—"

"That's not what I meant."

Odie stops, sits on a short rock wall on the edge of the street. He reaches out his good hand and I take it, then sit beside him. He inches closer so our shoulders are touching.

"My dad is kind of an egomaniac, and he just wants me to do everything he did. Take the same exact path, go to the same exact school . . . it's like he doesn't even see me."

I think of my own dad, standing beside me at the inn, barely looking up from the computer. How sometimes he passes me in the apartment, his eyes unfocused, like he's lost in thought. It's so lonely, being with a parent like that.

"He basically got me into Yale—muscled me in," he says. "I know how absolutely gross that sounds, and trust me—I feel gross about it."

"What do you mean, muscled you in?"

"Since it's his alma mater. He's made hundreds of thousands in donations every year, and increased the donations in the years leading up to me applying," he says. "And what's really frustrating is he doesn't think I know about it. Like I'm dumb or something."

It *is* really gross. More than anything, it feels unfair. I think back to the college admissions scandal I'd heard about in the news, where that consultant was creating fake athletic profiles and helping kids cheat on their SATs to get them into Ivy League schools. Yale, Princeton, Columbia . . . those colleges have always felt out of reach for public school kids on the island. We only had about forty kids in our graduating class at Avalon High School, and none of them got into Ivy Leagues—it was a huge win that Pita even got into UC Santa Cruz.

What's the point, though, of getting good grades and doing everything right when the system is stacked against you? When you don't have the money or resources to apply to thirty schools or send in donations to bolster your application?

"You're disgusted," Odie says.

He must have read my expression.

"Not necessarily by you. You obviously know it's wrong."

"Trust me, I know," he says. "And the worst part is, I have good grades. I did well at a top-tier private school and I got into UCLA on my own. The right way. My dad thinks I shouldn't go there. . . . I just want to choose my own path. I deserve to choose my own path."

"Everyone does, but not everyone gets to."

I'm not sure who we're talking about now—him or me. The last year has made me feel so out of control of my own life, like I got swept up in a riptide and it's useless to do anything but let it take me. I don't know how to get back on course now.

"You seem like you understand," he says.

"Kind of. I mean, my dad didn't get me into Yale," I say. "He didn't really want me to go away to school, even if I had been able to get my applications together. If it were up to him, I'd stay and help with the inn—that's always been his preference. I mean, it was good enough for him, staying on Catalina. Spending his whole life here. Also, we took a big hit after Covid and we never really recovered. Things have only gotten worse."

"That's hard."

"And everyone else is going to college, but that doesn't feel right. Even culinary school or something . . . it feels really far off. Like a pipe dream."

"What would you do, if you could do anything?" he says.

"That's a dangerous question."

"What? Why?"

"Because I can't just do anything."

I don't have unlimited resources, unlimited funds. It almost feels cruel, to ask me to dream like that, when I don't have a way of making those dreams happen. But however annoyed I am by the question, it breaks when Odie covers my hand with his. He's just holding it there, waiting for me to respond, his brown eyes full and innocent.

He really wants to know.

"I'm not sure . . ." I say.

But the question has already worked its way inside me. Ideas are percolating; possibilities are taking shape whether I want them to or not. It's scary to think about, but it's also hopeful . . . something I haven't felt in a long, long time.

I already know it was a gift—his asking.

FIFTEEN

THE SECOND WEEK WITH ODIE

"Maybe I should get you ice," I say, turning to look up at the inn, towering on the cliff above us. We stayed on Pebbly Beach Road and walked all around to the beach below room 2, but Odie is holding his knuckles in his hand, rubbing them every so often.

"Isn't that high risk at this point? With your dad manning the lobby?"

"It's definitely not ideal."

There'd be questions. Why am I home before the fireworks, why am I alone, what happened to Pita, and what do I need the ice for? There's a chance there's some in the apartment, but I haven't made any in months and my dad never makes any. It would be kind of sad to return with three measly pieces in a Ziploc.

"I have an idea," I say.

I grab his good hand and lead him down to the water.

We climb over the rocky beach—the same beach where we first met. The ocean is usually just below seventy degrees at this point in the summer. Not icy, but maybe cool enough to stave off the swelling. I hike my dress up around my legs and wade in with him, but it proves to be impossibly awkward, with him hunched down to keep his hand in.

"I have a better idea," I say.

"I like this," he says, following me back up the beach like a puppy. I stop just beyond the spot where the waves crash onto the shore. "I give myself over to your ideas."

I hike my skirt up again and kneel, pushing away rocks until I hit sand and water. I build a basin, like I used to when I was kid, going as far down as I can. Then I sit back and Odie plops his hands inside.

"So . . . ?" I say after a minute.

"I think it's working. My hand is legitimately cold."

"All of me is legitimately cold. I think that's one of the downsides of the ocean."

The skin on my arms and legs is covered in goose bumps, and even though I'm holding my elbows, trying to shield myself against the wind, it does little to help. Out ahead of us, one of the cruise ships is having a massive party on one of the upper floors. Even from where we're sitting, we can see strobe lights and people dancing beyond the windows.

"When you asked me before about what I would do if I could do anything," I say. "I've always wanted to open a food truck. Or really . . . a dessert truck."

"Whoa . . . cool," he says.

"Lenora has been teaching me more and more techniques—I'm actually supposed to work with her tomorrow morning. I don't know that I need some formal culinary school. If I keep practicing and experimenting, I might be able to just test it out."

"It does seem like something that would work . . . especially if you have a good Instagram page to sell it."

"Right?"

"That's really cool," he says.

"What about you? You didn't answer your own question."

I rest my cheek on my arm, so I'm facing him.

"I used to have a lot of ideas about what I wanted to do. Some of it kid stuff, like being a firefighter or whatever. But I don't know . . ." he says, pulling at a curl in the front of his hair. "Lately it's gotten hard to separate my parents' voices from my own. It's like I don't even know what I want anymore, because what they want feels so much more pressing."

"It's not."

"It doesn't feel that way."

"I get it . . . it's not logical."

"UCLA seems like the next right thing. If I could just convince my dad to let me go there . . . maybe, I don't know. I could get my life back on course."

"Right now you're still on a detour."

"The biggest detour."

"The *greatest* detour . . ." I say, and he smiles.

His shoulders keep shaking ever so slightly, like he has the shivers.

"This is silly," he finally says. "My hand will be okay. We should just go inside."

Inside.

Meaning into the quiet, abandoned hotel room he's been staying in. Where there's a big queen-sized bed and a door with a lock. Where we're far away from the other rooms, right by the ocean, surrounded by the sound of the water crashing onto the shore . . .

"What about the fireworks? They should start any second. I bet the cruise ship will set some off. . . ."

I want to see them and I don't want to see them. I'm just honestly afraid of what might happen if Odie and I are alone together, far away from the rest of the world. From anything that matters. One thing is clear—I'm falling for him.

It's a fast, helpless spiral.

The kind that could destroy me if I'm not careful.

"Oh, right. Yeah, we should wait for the fireworks," he says.

He keeps his hand in the ocean water and stares up at the sky. I wonder if he's noticed how different the stars are here—pinpricks of perfect light. The winds blow cold and fierce on the island, clearing the smog that blots out everything in LA.

I stare up at the sky too. Every now and then he turns and looks at me, and it's like I can feel his eyes on my skin, tracing the outline of my legs, crusted with sand. At some point the thin strap of my dress fell off my shoulder. He reaches over and puts it back. Then he pats it in place and laughs.

His fingers on my bare skin is almost too much.

"I don't know if I can wait . . ." I say without thinking.

"I don't think I can either . . ."

But we wait there, the sound of the ocean roaring past us.

He raises his hand out of the basin. It's dripping. He turns it above my bare knee so his fingers just barely graze my kneecap. We both watch as two thick drops fall. They twist down the side of my calf, until they slip past my ankle.

Just the feel of it and I suck in a sharp inhale.

"It's freezing out here," I say, not looking away from him.

He leans in, whispering.

"I want to kiss you but I'm afraid someone might see."

"I'm afraid someone might see too."

The back part of the dining room faces this beach. The lights are still on, and every now and then I see Araceli's pony-tail zip past. The French couple I checked in earlier today is sitting at a table by the windows, finishing up their dinner.

It's like Odie and I are both under some spell, fixed in place. I'm the one to break it first. I stand and turn back to the room. It feels dangerous . . . reckless, even.

"We should probably go inside," I say. "To warm up."

"To warm up." he repeats.

He follows me back up the beach, to where I find the spare key and unlock the door. Every time I step inside, it looks different—warmer, more his. He's put the few items he's bought in a folded pile on the ledge beneath the window. The lantern sits on the small round table. He goes to it and turns it on, filling the room with a golden light. I immediately move to the window, making sure the curtain is pulled across it.

His eyes find mine, his face serious.

Oh my god . . . what have I done?

"I see you've been keeping yourself occupied," I say, playfully picking up the romance novel from off his bed. There's a dog ear toward the back now.

"I have to read something," he says. "Otherwise I just spend all day thinking about this girl I just met. And that's not good for anyone. I don't want her to feel any pressure, like she's become my whole world. . . ."

"I bet she'd be flattered to even be thought of that way."

He moves toward me and sits on the edge of the bed. Grabs my hand and pulls me toward him, so I'm standing between his legs. His right hand is still freezing and wet from the ocean water. When he runs it along my arm all the tiny hairs stand up in its wake.

"This isn't just a game to me," I say, barely able to get the words out.

"It's not a game to me either."

"I'm serious—you're going to leave. And I'll be stuck here."

"You're not stuck."

"I am."

He keeps shaking his head. Then he stands, holding my face in his hands. He's so much taller than me he has to stoop to look in my eyes.

"I wouldn't mess with you like that. I wouldn't do what he did," he says, and his voice has an edge to it. "I'm not like that. I just . . . you're different, Callie. You're different, and this island is different. I feel like myself here. I don't know what it is, or why it makes sense . . . but I'll stay as long as that's okay with you."

"You said you'd stay forever."

"I want to stay forever."

It's not a question anymore, just an answer. I raise my lips to meet his and we are kissing. Our tongues find each other, our mouths moving together, and I kiss down his neck. His breaths are hot in my ear, sending me reeling. When he raises his hand to my back to unhook my bra I don't stop him. I want him to feel me—all of me.

To know me.

One of the straps of my dress slips off my shoulder. He tugs the top down and it all falls away—my bra, the dress— until I'm standing in front of him in my underwear. I have on a pink thong I've had for years. I'm about to say something about it—about how I wasn't expecting this, not really— when he leans down and finds my gaze again.

"You are so crazy beautiful."

He lands another kiss, so gently. Then his hands are on me, and my body is screaming with pleasure, wanting him to find every inch of me. When I finally take a breath I pull back, resting my forehead against his chest.

"I've never had sex before," I say. "And I don't want to now—I can't."

"No, we shouldn't," he says. "We don't have to do anything, Callie. If I can just be with you tonight . . . just hold you. That would be enough."

"Well, I should at least get to touch you, right?" I laugh.

I run my hands up his stomach muscles, so hard and smooth against my palms. He smiles as he tugs off his shirt and I press myself against him, letting our bodies touch for the first time. The closer I am to him the more he smells like himself—like some other place I haven't been to yet.

The air pops with sudden fireworks. The faint color flickers in the window, painting the light pink and green. He doesn't even register them—instead his hand is on my face again, his thumb brushing over my lips, my cheek. For a moment I can feel him against my leg, but he adjusts, stepping away. Then kisses me, much harder this time.

Outside, I hear the ocean, loud as a freight train— reassuring us it's still there.

SIXTEEN

THE THIRD WEEK WITH ODIE

It's so dark in room 2 it's hard to know what time it is. It's only when I catch the light on the floor, the perfect rectangle casting down from the window, that I realize we've overslept.

Or really—*I've* overslept.

"Oh shit," I say, sitting up in bed.

Odie is still asleep, his black hair a mess of curls. I have to physically slide out from under his arm to get up, and as soon as I do he opens his eyes.

"Stay . . . more cuddles . . ." He reaches out, tugging me back toward the mattress. "Don't leave. . . ."

"Do you know what time it is? Have you seen my phone?"

I'm searching the floor in the dim light. I find my bra and pull on my dress. I try to comb out my hair with my fingers, but every half an inch they get caught on a knot. I'm not sure how late we were up. Everything seems to slow here, the minutes bleeding together even more than they normally do on the island. After we made out, Odie lay beside me, running his fingers along my stomach, drawing circles around my belly button. We talked for hours about what it would be like tomorrow, and the next day . . . with him here, on the island. I fell asleep nestled in the dip of his arm.

"I think it's on the table?" he says, rubbing the sleep from his eyes. "Everything okay?"

He's right. It's on the table.

And I was supposed to be upstairs twenty minutes ago.

"I'm interning with Lenora this morning. She was going to teach me about meringues—she's doing a special dessert tonight."

"Oh no . . ."

I brush off my skirt and grab my sandals from under the bed. The light has shifted, and there's a long golden line across Odie's back. He looks perfect—almost too perfect. I don't want to leave him here.

"I'll come find you later. Or you can come find me. I'll be around in the afternoon."

"You sure? What about your dad?" he asks.

I'm not sure it matters anymore, because there's a very real chance he looked in my room last night and realized I never came home. Sophomore and junior year I'd sometimes crash at Pita's, since our parents have known each other for so long. But I haven't done that in ages, and definitely not recently. Not without permission.

"Actually, I'll come find you," I say.

"If I'm not here I'll be working on the boat."

Just the mention of the boat stops me. Does that mean he's still thinking of leaving? Why does he have to fix the boat?

"It has to get fixed even if I stay. I can't just leave it there," he says, as if reading my expression. "And I don't have much else to do . . . besides reading that romance novel. . . ."

He reaches out his hand, stretching toward me. I take a few steps and grab it. Then he pulls me down to the mattress one last time, squeezing me tight to his chest.

"I want to say something but I'm not going to say it. It might get weird," he whispers.

There's a long pause, and I'm not sure if he's joking. I think I know what the something is, because I feel it too, hovering just below the surface. But am I being delusional? How is it even possible, to care so much about someone you only met a couple of weeks ago?

"What is it?" I say, but I don't look at him.

"I'll tell you later."

I try to get up but he pulls me down one more time, landing a flurry of kisses on my head and cheeks. Then, with a woeful sigh, he lets me go.

When I finally get up to the kitchen, Lenora has the electric mixer going, letting it whip the egg whites into stiff peaks. It's so loud she doesn't even look up until I'm right beside her.

"What happened to you?" she says, switching it off.

"What do you mean?"

I grab my apron from the hook behind the door, and give a wave to Paul, who's washing dishes. Lenora raises her brow at him, like *Do you believe this one?*

"You look like you just rolled out of bed . . . and maybe didn't even change from last night? Where is this dress from?"

Now she leans in, studying every part of me. In the fluorescent lights I can see the places where the beer hit me. It's not super obvious, but it's there, and now I'm certain I stink like a bar. There are also stains around the skirt—not stain stains, but the places where it touched the ocean last night have this weird ring on them. I'd stupidly thought I didn't have to change . . . but now I realize I was wrong.

"Please just don't say anything to my dad?"

Lenora tucks a piece of graying hair behind her ear. She has it back in a low ponytail, but one strand always falls loose—sometimes she pins it with a bobby pin. She wipes her hands on the front of her apron and wraps me in a big hug.

"I wouldn't dare," she finally says. "You know he's just worried about you, right? It broke our hearts, seeing you so upset about that guy. You deserve so much better."

Does she know I was with a guy? Lenora sees through a lot of my bullshit, but it is possible I was just out getting drunk with friends last night, which is what half the kids in my high school were doing. How does she know I wasn't getting into some other kind of trouble?

"You don't need to worry—I'm fine," I say.

"I just want to meet him, or her, or whoever it is."

Then she goes back to the electric mixer, checking the peaks of the meringue. I'm staring at the side of her face, trying to figure out how she even knew there's a guy.

"What?" she says. "Your hair gave it away. That's make-out hair—it's very obvious. Oh, you have this whole *I'm lit from within* thing going on. Like, *I'm walking on clouds!*"

"No way."

"I'm going to give you unsolicited advice, Cal," she says.

"Please."

"Tell your dad as soon as possible. I'll be there as a buffer, if you need me to be. You just don't want him to find out on his own. It won't be good. I can promise you that."

"I was hoping he wouldn't find out at all."

"It's been months. You're allowed to date again."

It never even occurred to me to tell my dad about Odie. I'd kind of decided I'd never talk to him about a guy ever again, after we had the long awkward conversation about Harper and what happened. Pita's mom had called him first and given him the rundown on everything, saying that she had a responsibility to him—that she had to tell him the truth. She said she'd want him to do the same for her, if he knew anything like that about Pita. I'd cried and begged, but she was never going to do anything but the right thing.

People with integrity, *amirite*?

"I guess maybe I could . . ." I say, thinking out loud.

"Is it someone you want in your life? For real?"

"Yeah. . . ."

I feel all the color rush to my cheeks. Even if Lenora is technically just a friend, it's still a little embarrassing, discussing boys and stuff with her.

"Then do it—I'm telling you." She flicks the electric mixer on again, then signals to a shelf on the other side of the kitchen. "Now will you get me the cornstarch?" she yells over its roar.

Why did I follow Lenora's advice? Why was I so incredibly dumb, thinking my dad would somehow be chill and open and ready to meet someone I was dating? Why would I think this wouldn't go anything but horribly?

Odie is sitting in my rolling desk chair, complete with a fuzzy pink throw pillow. It's the only other chair in the entire apartment that can fit around our tiny dining table. My dad bought the table off a neighbor years ago—it's barely more than two feet wide. Now it's layered with sub wrappers, a container of pickles, and potato chip bags. When I tried to tell my dad maybe we should do something besides subs for dinner, since Odie has never been here and all, he said it would be fine.

"Yale is impressive," my dad says, blotting some mustard from the corner of his mouth. "Your parents must be thrilled. I'm thrilled, and I just met you."

"They are."

Odie glances sideways at me, looking for understanding.

"What? What's behind that?" my dad asks, noticing.

"Nothing," I say quickly.

But Odie takes a deep breath, says, "I wanted to go to UCLA, though, so I don't know. . . ."

"You don't know what?" My dad looks from me back to Odie, unsure what he's missing.

"Nothing," Odie says.

He takes another bite of his turkey sub and we all chew in silence. It's excruciating. I can hear my dad eating every potato chip and cracking the spine of every pickle. Odie has been here an hour and I keep seeing the apartment the way he must see it. How one couch cushion sags in the center, because my dad is the only one who sits on it and he always sits in the same exact spot. I never realized our lampshades are so dirty, but they are—crusted with dust—the lightbulbs too. Even the blinds offend me somehow. When we upgraded the rest of the window treatments at the inn we didn't have money to do ours, so we still have the gray vertical vinyl ones from a decade ago.

"Odie is a really impressive sailor. He races boats," I say.

"Where at?" my dad asks.

"California Yacht Club, mostly."

Just the way my dad puts down his sandwich, I can tell he's uncomfortable. I'm not sure how much it costs to be a member there but I imagine it's phenomenally expensive. All of this—Yale, yacht clubs, an eighteen-year-old on an extended vacation, on his own, with no end date in sight . . . it's not something he's encountered a lot.

I mean, neither have I.

"I'm really only okay—it's not that interesting," Odie says, as if noticing. "But this place . . . it's really cool. I keep telling Callie, Catalina seems like an amazing place to grow up."

My dad relaxes back in his chair, sighs. "You know? It is. I've spent my whole life here. My parents opened the inn in the seventies, and then I took it over."

"So this is where you met Callie's mom?" Odie asks.

Now I'm uncomfortable. When I invited Odie to meet my dad, we agreed on a story about why he was here and where he was staying. We talked through all the obvious land mines—what if he asked for Odie's last name? What if he wanted to know how we met? But I never considered Odie would ask about my mom . . . it's not really something my dad and I ever talk about.

For years after she died we had pictures of her everywhere, and Lenora would talk about her constantly, so it didn't feel as weird. There were photo strips on the fridge and framed pictures on the walls from when I was a baby, and a few of all three of us at the beach. When I was twelve, my dad briefly dated a woman named Carol—she runs a nature camp on the other side of the island. That's when things shifted. The framed photos were swapped out, the photo strips moved to the corkboard in my room. Lenora said it was natural, that my dad had to at least try to date again. But a door closed then and it hasn't opened since.

"Yes, actually," my dad says, and he looks down to hide a smile. "She grew up in Orange County, and she was just here visiting for the summer. Callie's mom had all this energy. She was super creative and interested in so many things, and at the time she'd been really into photography."

"Photography?" I ask. I knew my mom was visiting Catalina that summer, but I had no idea what she was doing here. I guess I'd always assumed she'd just rented a place and was enjoying the beach, the ocean.

"I have the photographs somewhere," my dad says. "I'll have to find them. . . ."

"So she came here to take photographs?" Odie asks.

He's leaning in now, and I can tell he's genuinely interested. And maybe even a little excited, to hear that my parents met the same way we did—that my mom was a visitor and my dad was a local. That sometimes just one summer can change everything.

"There are these fish—the garibaldi fish," my dad says. "They're native to the kelp forests off the coast of Catalina. If you're down by the ferry docks, you just have to go to the side and you'll see them. There are these fish food machines—like candy machines—and you can feed them there. And your mother—"

He turns to me as he says it, and I swear there's a tiny sparkle in his eyes—a light I haven't seen in a long time.

"Your mother was into underwater photography back then," he says. "Specifically contrasts. So instead of photographing tropical fish in beautiful tropical waters, she liked the contrast of the garibaldi fish."

"They're this electric orange color," I explain to Odie. "We call them Catalina goldfish. It's like they glow."

"Rad," Odie says.

"And everyone loves the kelp forests, but if we're being honest, they're kind of—"

"Drab." I laugh.

Then my dad smiles. "You said it."

"They are! That's a very unpopular opinion, though," I add.

"Because they are really rich in ocean life. And they are beautiful, in their own way. I think Callie just means it's kind of like swimming in a giant pool of seaweed. Or moss or something," my dad says. "But Callie's mom loved it, because the photographs were high in contrast—these orange fish against this blue-green, brownish background. And she'd mess with the contrast and turn the photographs into these art pieces. Had a bunch of gallery shows in town."

"Wait . . . she sold them?" I ask.

"For a bit, yes," my dad says.

How did I not know any of this? When Lenora talks about my mom, she usually tells stories about her floral shop (she was a florist for five years) or the dive boat they worked on together. I've even heard stories about them getting drunk at the beach club and going skinny-dipping after. But art galleries and photographs? Never.

"And I was in town, picking up a shipment for the inn, and I don't know why . . . I was just kind of drawn to this gallery up on Vernon Ave. I'd lived here my whole life and I'd never set foot inside. And I saw a bunch of people in there drinking wine—"

"You don't even drink," I say.

"I know, I know," my dad says. "But I just felt like I had to go in. And then I met your mom, and then from that point on we were inseparable. She kept extending her stay by a few days, then a few more. She could never bring herself to leave."

Odie's eyes meet mine and he smiles, all dimples. The story does feel familiar—even I can admit that. I try not to get carried away by it, by this idea that maybe Odie and I have something in common with my parents. That we could fall in love and last decades or more.

It's tempting, though. . . .

My dad goes on, and tells Odie a bit about the inn and why he's always loved running it, and I'm surprised when he mentions business hasn't been great the past few years. It's like at a certain point he forgot he was supposed to be making a good impression with Odie, and instead he just starts telling the truth. It's strange, but refreshing, when he starts doing an impression of the uptight guest who was ranting yesterday about the "crunchiness" of the pool towels. Odie and I laugh so much my eyes start watering.

After we finish the freezer ice cream sandwiches my dad and I are obsessed with, it's late. My dad looks exhausted, the circles under his eyes more pronounced than they normally are. It's like he's been holding up the sky lately . . . or our very own patch of it.

"I should really get back," Odie finally says.

"It was great meeting you, son." My dad gives him a handshake and half hug.

"You too, Mr. Quinn," Odie says. "I hope to see you soon."

I walk him out to the front parking lot, checking to make sure no one is at the lobby doors. After a successful dinner with my dad, the last thing we need is someone seeing him sneaking down steps on the side of the inn. We could pretend he's taking a shortcut to the beach if anyone asks . . . but I really don't want anyone to ask.

Odie hugs me tight, burying his face into my neck.

"Your dad is great," he says.

"My dad is okay," I whisper.

"Stop."

"This is actually the best dinner we've had together in a really long time."

"All it took was the guy you're dating who you're not supposed to be dating," Odie says. He kisses me once, checking to make sure my dad isn't looking out the window, watching us. "I better quit while I'm ahead."

"Good idea."

But I give him an extra kiss, unable to stop myself.

When I get back inside, my dad has already tossed the trash from dinner and is sitting in his usual spot on the couch, working on one of his sudoku books. He started doing them during Covid, to relieve stress, and he hasn't stopped. We have a whole stack of them in the bookcase because he likes to keep the finished ones for posterity.

"I'm surprised you like him," I say. "You don't like anyone."

"Who said I like him?" my dad deadpans. But then he smiles.

"That was nice."

"He's very impressive. He clearly adores you. And he had the decency to introduce himself, not like some of the boys you've dated in the past. . . ." My dad taps the edge of his pen on the top of the book, as if he's considering whether to say something. "I'm just worried, Callie."

"You don't have to—"

"What's going to happen when he leaves at the end of the summer? I don't want you getting your heart broken. It was hard these past few months . . . and I can tell Odie is different, but—"

"It's okay, Dad," I say, an edge in my voice.

Then I slip past him, into my room, relieved when the door clicks shut behind me. We just had a nice night—the first one where we even talked in a long time. I hate that he had to bring up what happened with Harper. This is totally different.

As soon as I'm alone, though, his question comes back. What's going to happen when Odie leaves at the end of the summer? Did I really think he would stay on Catalina forever? He has parents and a college he's committed to. No matter what he wants or what he says, he has to go back. His bar mitzvah money won't last more than a few more months.

And yet . . . everything in me wants this. Us.

It doesn't make any sense, but I don't care.

What am I going to do when he leaves?

The answer comes to me, as simple and clear as ever: I'm going to love him.

The way I do now. Always.

SEVENTEEN

THE THIRD WEEK WITH ODIE

I stare down at the ocean floor, pointing to the garibaldi fish below. There's only one, all alone, and it floats through the kelp, weaving a slow, lazy *S*. Odie gives me a thumbs-up, which feels like something a grandpa might do, but it's our only way to communicate while snorkeling. I try to smile under my mask.

Eventually I pop back to the surface. He tugs his mask off and bobs along next to me.

"Garibaldi fish—check," I say.

"They are really beautiful. I'm glad we waited."

"It's different seeing them now, after what my dad said."

"This is going to sound dumb . . . but I honestly didn't know this was here."

"Catalina?" I smirk.

"No." He laughs. "I knew Catalina was here. But it's like

this whole other world. It's its own paradise. I can't believe you got to grow up here."

"Yeah . . . it is cool."

When I stare up at the cliffs above, then the ocean stretching out in front of us, it does feel really special. Preserved in a way Los Angeles isn't and never could be.

We swim into the shallows, where we can stand. The water on the island is this vivid turquoise—like something out of a travel magazine. Sure, the kelp interrupts it in places, but that only adds to the beauty. We peel everything off—flippers and wet suits—until we're back to our bathing suits. My skin is happy, relieved, to be in the sun and fresh breeze. I'm standing there, squeezing the ocean out of my hair, when Odie comes up behind me, pulling me close to him.

"The only bad thing about snorkeling is I couldn't be near you," he says.

"You were, like, four feet away the whole time."

"Not close enough."

I spin around to face him, rest my hands behind his neck. He's still dripping wet, the little droplets running down his temples and cheeks. He's being dramatic, but the more time I spend with him the more I understand what he means. I always want to be right here, right in his arms, so close we're touching.

He picks me up and squeezes me, gives me a long, slow

kiss, letting his lips linger there, then he kisses down my neck. He grabs my hand as we walk up the narrow strip of shore, our wet suits slung over our shoulders.

"There's not really a beach here, but we could go into town and hang out," I say.

"I'm already addicted to Sailor's. It's a constant craving now."

"I mean . . . they import their ice cream. They're really serious."

I'm maneuvering the steps, the snorkels around my arm, when I hear voices above me. Pita and Marlowe, another girl from our high school who's going to UC Irvine in a few weeks, are there, sitting at the stone picnic tables across the way. They have their towels and a giant bag with snorkels and things. I walk by the LOVER'S COVE sign listing all the beach rules. As I cross the street, our eyes meet, but then Pita looks away.

Odie climbs the stairs behind me. Normally I'd just introduce them—he's already met my dad, anyway—but Pita keeps on talking to Marlowe, like I'm not even there. We've exchanged a few texts over the past two weeks, but I never really checked in after Zeke left. It wasn't this conscious choice I made, to ghost. . . . I kind of figured Pita would be busy getting ready for Santa Cruz and college. Besides, there's only so much I can contribute to conversations about dorm room setups and class schedules. No one needs me to weigh in on fall break or whether they should study abroad for a semester.

"Hey . . ." I say when I reach them.

"Hey." Pita just kind of nods.

"Everything cool?" I ask.

Pita looks at me, then back at Odie, who's just climbed the last step behind me.

"I don't know . . . is everything cool?" Pita asks. "I haven't heard from you in weeks and then someone told me you got into a fistfight?"

"Wait . . . what?"

It takes me a beat to even process what she's saying. So much has happened since Odie hit Brett—it feels like that was years ago. I don't know how to respond, really, or how to explain that the way it happened, he wasn't really in the wrong.

Not in the way I think of it, anyway.

Turns out I don't need to. Pita is already pushing past us and heading down the stairs, Marlowe in her wake. I've always liked Marlowe fine—she graduated second in our class and was in every club and all the honor societies (even silly ones, like Latin Honor Society). But she's never even made out with anyone, and she definitely wasn't the nicest to me in May, when the story of my selfie debacle spread. In her mind, Topless Selfie equals Bad Judgment, and probably some Sluttiness too.

It's not helping my case that Odie is still holding my hand.

Shirtless, soaking-wet Odie.

"Bye, Callie," Marlowe says as she heads down the steps.

"Bye. . . ."

Then I watch as they walk up the beach, their snorkeling gear dangling from each hand. It only takes a few steps before they're chatting to each other. Laughing and smiling again.

Like that never even happened.

"What was that about?" Odie asks as we start back up the road.

"That was my best friend, Pita."

"Best friend? I thought you barely knew that girl."

"Things have been weird lately." I turn, watching as Pita and Marlowe sink into the water. They're just barely visible, their bare shoulders shining in the sun. "It feels like we have less and less in common . . . and I don't know."

"You don't know what?" he asks.

"It's just hard. It feels like everything's changing."

Odie makes a visor with his hand. He bought a pair of sunglasses from a tourist shop on Crescent but they only lasted two days before one of the screws came out, and now he goes everywhere like this, squinting against the sun.

"She's going away to school?" he asks.

I nod, and everything feels heavy suddenly. Now I'm wondering if it's petty that I don't want to talk about college all the time. It's not that I'm not happy for Pita, it's that I've been talking about it for months already and can't imagine that this is what the next four years are going to be like for us. The gulf between us is only growing.

Maybe it's better that she has Marlowe, so they can go through the whole experience together.

"How long have you known each other?" Odie asks.

"Since fourth grade."

He tilts his head to the side, thinking. Then he drops my hand. I'm sure that he's judging me, that I have been really petty. Maybe he's even going to call me out on it. But instead he wraps his arm around my shoulder and pulls me close, squeezing me in a hug as we walk.

"That is really hard," he says.

We keep walking like that, and my hand finds his again, our fingers knitting back together. For once I don't feel the need to explain anything or justify how I feel.

It's obvious Odie just gets it . . . and me.

"You don't get to do that," I say.

But Odie squirms away, hiding his face in his hands. We're lying on one of my old blankets, this one dotted with little Descendants icons. We're still digesting the epic amount of ice cream we consumed. The sun is low, the beach much emptier now. Behind us, on the main strip, everyone's looking for a place to eat dinner.

"Tell me." I say.

"It's actually too embarrassing."

"That's the whole point of your most embarrassing

moment," I say. "I just told you about how I said 'BYE, LOVE YOU' to a cashier, who happened to be the hottest senior boy at my high school."

Odie peeks out from behind his fingers. I prop my head on my hand so I'm watching his every move.

"Fine," he says. "Fine."

"Don't act like you're doing me some favor. We made a deal . . . mine for yours."

His cheeks are actually getting red—real, tomato red. He takes a deep breath, then starts talking, his eyes still closed against the setting sun.

"So when I was eleven I had braces, and I was really small for my age," he says. "I looked like I was at least two years younger than everyone else. I was super scrawny too. At school, everyone had known me forever and it didn't matter as much. But I started this sleepaway camp and it was like—from day one, the older guys were just ruthless. They were always picking on me."

It's hard for me to think about Odie as someone who was ever picked on, but I can tell by his expression he's serious. He's cringing, like it's physically hurting him to think about.

"So for the camp talent show, I decide I'm going to play the guitar. Because I was playing a lot back then and I was pretty good, and I know people will think it's cool. I was going to do it acoustic and kind of riff on this old song I was obsessed with. I was convinced everyone would really see how cool I was, then I'd be, like, set for the rest of the summer."

"What song?" I ask.

"'Just Like Heaven'?"

I nod, because I know it . . . and I've always loved it too.

"I get to the mic, and I have the guitar strap on over my shoulder, and I've just started. But I don't even get three seconds into it before this older kid runs out from the wings and pants me. Underwear and everything."

"No. . . . Little Odie. . . . No. . . ."

I throw my arms around him, and now I'm cringing too.

"And because I'm holding the guitar, it takes me forever to get my shorts back up. I basically had to hop offstage with my butt facing the audience."

I kiss his face, hating to think of someone doing that to him. It's too cruel.

"What did you do? Did you leave early?" I finally ask.

"Oh, they called my parents. And I basically begged them to come get me and bring me home. I did not want to stay there."

"Good," I say.

"Not really . . . because it was the summer my mom was wedding planning and she didn't want me home. She said she had too much going on. And my dad was working nonstop so he was out."

"You had to stay?"

"Yeah."

There's sadness in his expression, but then he rubs his hand over his face, as if he can wipe it away. He gives me a smile.

"Not great," he says.

"No," I agree.

I obviously know it was wrong for Odie to just pick up and leave without telling his parents anything. But then he'll say something about them offhand, or tell a story about his childhood, and it will all feel kind of cold . . . like they thought of him as more of an accessory than their kid. His dad has only ever told him he loves him like three times in his whole life. It all just feels removed.

Odie shifts, then props his head on his hand to face me. Our other hands meet on the blanket, and he gives mine a squeeze.

"I would've been friends with you at camp," I say.

"I know."

"How?"

"You're just that kind of person."

He leans in and kisses me. It's slow at first, then he pulls me closer. We fall back against the blanket and he kisses me again, and I don't care that we're right near the main road and someone might see. I don't want this to end.

"Callie?" he asks, his voice soft.

"Odie . . ."

"I want to say something but I don't want it to freak you out."

His brown eyes search my face.

"Just say it," I tell him.

"I love you . . . and I know it's complicated, and there's a lot going on with me, but I'm sorry, I do. I fell in love with you."

"Don't be sorry," I say, and I'm already smiling. My whole body feels lit from the inside. I can't believe that this is real—that *we* are real. That Odie has been feeling all the same things I have this whole time. "I love you too. I don't know what that means for us, but I do."

His face breaks into the biggest smile, and he kisses me again, pulling me to him.

"And I've decided something," I say.

"That sounds so serious."

"It is? Kind of?" Strangely, this part feels even more nerve-racking to admit, but if we're going from moment to moment, letting things be what they are, then I have to say it. "I don't know what's going to happen either, but I know I want to lose my virginity to you. I want it to be with you."

"Are you sure?" Odie's lips curl into a smile.

"Yes."

He rests his palm on my cheek and kisses me again.

"I really do love you, Callie. I do," he says, but it's almost too insistent. There's something behind what he's saying, even if I can't figure out what. Is he worried about what happens next? That I'll get too attached? Is it too much responsibility for him?

I know that he has to leave eventually, that as much as he

says he'll stay forever, it's not realistic. But we could try long-distance . . . or even if he came back to visit . . .

"Don't worry about me," I say. "I'll be okay. I always am."

"I just don't want to hurt you."

"I know."

The rest feels hazy, like it's all happening in a dream. We gather up the blanket and hold hands as we walk to the convenience store just off Crescent. Eli Parker's mom works there, so I hang in the back, looking at the different chip options while Odie goes to the counter to get condoms. The television screen above the counter plays a car insurance commercial.

I feel heady, light, like I'm floating through each moment. I have on a long dress over my bathing suit from this morning, and there's still sand stuck to my legs and nestled in my hair. This is how I've always pictured losing my virginity—with someone I love, who loves me, on one of my favorite beaches on the island. It's impossible to know what will happen next, but we'll always have this night together.

Odie is paying for the condoms when the commercial ends and the KTLA news starts up again. The anchorwoman is blond, with thick fake eyelashes. "Tonight we have an urgent request from Salvador Reyes, the Hollywood producer who gave us the popular action films *Back from the Edge* and *The Last Days in Mexico City*. His son, Odysseus Reyes, has been missing since taking his boat out three weeks ago."

The news cuts to a press conference, with a handsome fiftysomething man at the mic. Behind him, a thin white woman and a girl about my age are watching, their eyes puffy and red. They put up a picture of . . . Odie? No. Then Salvador says something about Odysseus's mother and girlfriend, gesturing to the two people behind him.

Odysseus Reyes.

His mother and *girlfriend*.

That's all I need to hear.

Odie has turned away from the counter and is coming toward me, panicked. I can already see him holding up his hands, like he can explain, but there's no explaining this.

It's already too late for him—and for us.

EIGHTEEN

THE THIRD WEEK WITH ODIE

I push outside, the cool night air prickling my skin. I don't realize I'm running until I am, up the long meandering path back to the inn.

"Callie!" he calls out behind me. "Callie, please! Wait!"

He's faster than I am and he closes the gap between us. When he reaches for my arm I shake him off. But then he runs in front of me to block the path.

"Get out of the way, *Odysseus*," I say.

"I can explain."

"You don't have to. You lied about everything."

I start laughing as I say it, but I can feel the white-hot rage behind my eyes, threatening to spill over. It is almost too ridiculous, too unbelievable. I get lying about who his father is. But it's too much, to not even mention his girlfriend, to not mention ever dating anyone, really.

"Do you think I'm stupid? You think I'm some dumb

local girl you can just lie to and dump? Is that what this is?" My voice breaks as I say it and I turn away, not wanting him to see the tears that are coming hot and fast.

"No . . . that's not it at all. . . ."

"So what is it, *Odysseus*? What is it, then?"

When I turn back he's tearing up too. He keeps pressing his fingers to his eyes, like that could stop him from crying.

"You have a girlfriend," I say. "I was about to lose my virginity to someone who has a girlfriend. Can you even imagine how that makes me feel?"

"She's not my girlfriend."

"Who is she, then?"

I feel a tug in the pit of my stomach—I still want to believe him. *Tell me something that makes sense*, I think, watching as his expression shifts. *Tell me something I can hang on to.*

But he just stands there, silent.

"Why would I believe anything you say? Why?" I ask.

A young family walks past, pushing a double stroller. On instinct, the man grabs his wife, pulling her away from us. He's one of the guests from the inn—they checked in yesterday—so I hide my face, hoping he didn't recognize me.

"I'm sorry, Callie. I didn't handle it well. But I've never been in anything like this before. . . ."

"I don't need sorries."

Odie glances over my shoulder, at the bachelorette party that's heading toward us. The bride has one of those pink satin sashes on. He grabs my hand and pulls me down a side street, where there's an empty bench. It's supposed to be for people eating at the poke place, but no one is in there at this time of night.

"I knew if I told you my name," he starts, "you'd probably look it up online . . . and then who knows what you'd find. There's only one Odysseus in LA and it's me."

"Who says I was going to look you up?"

"People have. People do." He leans forward, resting his head in his hands. "Maybe I shouldn't have lied, but I didn't want you to see who my dad was. I didn't want you to know every movie and TV show he's produced before you knew anything about me. Is that crazy?"

It wasn't crazy. But it was dishonest.

"You're just hiding out," I say. "Using me."

"No."

"Yes, *Odysseus*, yes."

"I hate when you say it like that."

"I hate that you did this—you lied to me."

"She's not my girlfriend."

"According to the news she is."

"According to my parents she is—that's all."

"That's enough. I can't date someone with a girlfriend."

He grabs my hands and holds them to his chest. I'm physically annoyed by it—by this presumption he can touch me. That I'll want anything to do with him after this night.

"Her name is Pen. We grew up together. Our mothers are best friends, and it's all this messy, enmeshed mess," he says.

"But I broke up with her two weeks before I got here. We're not together anymore."

"Two whole weeks!"

I pull my hands away from him. It keeps getting worse . . . I'm basically his rebound. He broke up with his girlfriend, showed up here, and had a fling to make himself feel better.

I'm starting to wish I never met him.

That I hadn't even been working that night when the storm rolled in.

"It's been over for a long time," Odie says. "And honestly, it just feels like another thing I didn't really choose. It was more this thing I went along with, because everyone else felt so sure about it and I didn't know how to say no. We were only even dating a few months, but then suddenly she was talking about going to the same college as me."

I let my feet slide out from underneath me, my head falling onto the back of the bench. I hate hearing about Odie with anyone else. That he was even considering going to college with someone. I'm already in my head about it, coming up with a whole story about who this Pen girl is. How she must be so much smarter than me, so much better connected. I can't compete with someone going to Yale.

A tear slips down my temple. I don't even bother swiping it away.

"Listen to me, Callie," he says, trying to position himself so I'm looking right at him. "You have to listen to me. Here, on this island, I feel like myself again. It's like being with you has made me stronger. My head is finally clear.”

“I’m sure it is,” I say.

“Don’t do that. I’m serious.”

“I’m sure you are.”

Above us, the clouds shift, revealing the stars. I don’t want to even look at him, but he’s looking at me. He refuses to turn away. When I finally meet his gaze I see he’s crying too—that he at least seems really sorry. I don’t know if it even means anything now.

I don’t know if we can go back to how it was.

“This is what I want, Callie,” he insists. “This island. This summer. You.”

I feel my heart swell, the tears coming faster than before. When he reaches for my hand I let him take it, folding his fingers into mine. It’s so soft and warm.

“In every moment,” he says, “I’m choosing you.”

I want to believe him . . . but how can I?

How can I trust anything he says?

NINETEEN

I look like shit.

Utter and complete shit.

I stare into the foggy mirror, looking at my swollen, pink eyes. My blotchy cheeks. Even my hair looks sad, like I've been crying into it, the snot and tears causing some strands to stick together. After Odie and I sat on that bench for what felt like forever, I dragged myself back to the inn. He wouldn't leave my side. He kept saying he was sorry and he wished he could go back and do it all over again. I nearly closed the door in his face to get away, then retreated into my room for the night.

My dad was right. It's not even over yet—Odie hasn't even left—and this is already too much heartbreak. August will be here any day now, and he's going to leave, whether I want him to or not. He'll go on to Yale or UCLA or whichever school he decides will be perfect for him and I'll stay here, alone. He and Penelope will get back together, the cutest couple, and that will be it.

He'll barely even remember me.

My phone dings.

MATTY

UR DAD IS ASKING WHERE
U R

I must be late, but I don't know for sure and it's hard to care. I grab my wrinkled Ogygia Inn polo from the back of my desk chair and push outside and into the lobby, tying my hair back as I go.

"Whoa, you do not look good," Matty says as he holds the front door open for me.

"I'm aware."

"What happened?"

"Life."

I probably should've gotten a pair of sunglasses or something, to at least try to hide my face, but it's too late now. I sidle up to the lobby desk beside my dad. Thankfully he's lost in the computer system, his brows pinched together as he reviews today's arrivals.

"You're late," he says without looking up.

"Sorry."

Then he turns to me, studying the side of my face. I make myself busy organizing the extra toothpastes and floss in the desk drawer. I neaten the stack of Ogygia Inn notepads and slide them to the corner. I've wondered if my dad saw the news clip with Odie's face, but he's been working a ton, and I know he would've immediately texted me if he had.

"Are you okay?" he finally asks.

"Yep . . . fine."

I kneel down, opening another drawer and organizing the Ogygia Inn pens, waiting until he goes away. But weirdly . . . he doesn't. My dad just stands there.

"Did something happen with Odie?" he asks.

"I don't want to talk about it."

"Did he do something to you, Callie? Callie?"

His voice rises at the end, strained.

Did Odie do something to me? How bad is it, really? How much of the fault is his and how much of it is mine, for getting involved with him in the first place? He lied about what his commitments were back home—even if he and Penelope were broken up, he definitely didn't mention he'd just gotten out of a relationship. He let me believe certain things about us, when it was always going to come to this. His parents searching for him. Him having to go back.

There isn't such a thing as forever. Not for us.

"I think I'm just realizing you were right," I say.

"Oh . . ." My dad runs his hand over the back of his neck.

"Are you happy?"

"What? No, Callie." He shakes his head. "No."

A tween girl who checked in with her family yesterday

comes up to the desk, inquiring about paddleboard tours. I pull a brochure from the stack in the drawer and send her on her way. I think maybe that's enough to distract my dad—maybe now this conversation can end.

"Look," he says, staring down at the computer keys. "I know I've been hard on you this year. And it was disappointing, to see you just throw away your chance at college. I'd hoped you'd at least go through the process. Put a real effort in."

It stings, the way he phrases it. Did I throw away my chances? What's strange is I can relate to what Odie said . . . at certain times I felt like I was on this train, headed in a direction I never actually wanted to go in. It felt like I was just doing what everyone else was doing, even though that wasn't right for me. Is it possible this fall wasn't the worst thing to happen?

I have a chance now to figure out what I actually want for my future.

"But I saw how that boy looks at you . . . how he talks to you," my dad says. "If it's meant to be, it doesn't matter where either of you live or what he's doing next year. Haven't you ever heard that saying, what's meant for you won't miss you?"

I give him a tight-lipped smile. I hadn't heard that saying, but it's hard to believe it now, in the midst of all this. Even if Odie's story is true, and he really doesn't want to be with Pen and only lied because he was afraid of me having all these ideas about him . . . does it really matter?

He's going to leave, whether he loves me or not.

"Thanks, Dad," I say, just wanting the conversation to be over.

He gives me a side hug, awkwardly squeezing my shoulder, and disappears into his office. My shift is only just beginning, but the lobby seems sadder than it ever has before. The lights too bright, the guests more annoying than usual. I'm even a little annoyed with Matty, who texts me about the middle-aged couple from room 11 who keeps asking him where they can find "marijuana."

It's like Odie isn't even gone yet, and already my world is a little dimmer.

The sunset warms the dining room, painting the walls in yellow and oranges. As soon as my shift is over it's automatic. I find myself in the apartment, pulling off my sweaty polo and khakis, then changing into a clean sundress. I find myself swiping on lip gloss and brushing my hair, taking a breath and heading down the winding metal steps to the beach below.

I need to see him.

Maybe it's silly, because there's nothing else for him to say. There's nothing else we can do, even, now that his face has been plastered all over the news. Our hazy, timeless dream of summer is over and we have to face reality.

But I at least want to say goodbye.

When I get to the room I find the spare key and knock, but when I open the door he's not in there. The supplies are neatly stacked on the table. The lantern beside the leftover canned fruit and granola bars. The two blankets are folded on the mattress and I notice the romance novel sitting on the top of the dresser—where it was for ages before he found it.

My stomach is hollowed out, my feet unsteady.

Where is he? Did he leave already?

Is it possible he went without saying goodbye?

I take the stairs two at a time, then cross the road, my feet crunching on the pebbly beach below. I stay close to the edge of the street, and follow the narrow beach all the way around, passing the last sunbather, and then cresting the hill to where we hid Odie's boat. Within a few steps I see him—hunched over the stern. The tool kit is behind him and he's adjusting one of the screws. He turns, hearing me there.

His eyes are a mess—as pink and swollen as mine were this morning. He looks like he's had the same few days that I've had. Before I can take another step he's on his feet, holding his hands out in front of him.

"You're here," he says. "I can't believe you're here."

"Of course I am."

"I'm sorry, Callie—you can't even know how sorry I am," he says, twisting his fingers in his hair. "You shouldn't have found out like that. You deserved better and now I'm terrified I ruined everything between us, because I wasn't brave enough to just tell you everything from the start."

I was sure he had ruined everything between us, but

seeing him now, like this, I'm not so certain. That's the strangest part—when we're together it feels so clear. Nothing about us can be ruined. Nothing about us can be destroyed.

"This is real, Callie," he says, and when he comes toward me my whole body responds. "This is maybe the first real love I've ever had in my life. And I spent the last few days fixing the boat—if you want me to go, I will. I'll leave tomorrow. But that doesn't mean I can just stop loving you."

Then he waits, and now that it's my turn to speak I realize I only have one thing to say.

"I know . . ."

"You know . . . ?"

"I know this is real."

His expression shifts, the sadness gone. He's only a few feet from me now and he takes one slow step, then another, until he is unbearably close. I can see the last of the sun on his skin, can hear each of his trembling breaths. He rests his forehead on mine and we stand there, together, our hands finding the other's.

"I know this is real and I don't want you to go," I say.

"I don't want to go either."

I look into his eyes and I feel clear, stronger than I have in months. I'm starting to understand what I want—not just from Odie, but from life. It might not make sense to anyone else, but things are starting to make sense to me. And that's what matters.

"For as long as you're here, you're mine," I say.

"Of course I am."

That smile, those dimples. He lands kiss after kiss on my lips, tender at first, but then I return them. Our mouths move together, his tongue finding mine. He stops only for a breath to repeat it, making sure I heard it—that I know it by heart.

"I love you, Callie," he says. "I am so in love with you."

His hands are on me then, one bringing me closer, the other trailing down my neck and to the side of my body, where his thumb grazes my nipple under my dress. Everything in me wants him. And more than anything, I want to believe in this, to believe in love. That there are people who are meant for us—experiences we can't escape.

I pull him farther onto the secluded beach, where the cliffs block us on both sides. The sun has dipped low in the sky. The guests don't like this beach because of how rocky it is. The few who do explore never come back here after the breeze blows in, the air brisk and cool. I feel safe, protected, when I peel the dress over my head.

"We don't have to do this if you don't want—"

"I want to," I say.

Odie stares at me, then holds my face in his hands. "I want to, too. So much."

We fumble to the ground. Beside the boat he has his dry bag and the tool kit I lent him, but there's no blankets, no anything. We find a patch of smooth sand and he settles on top of me, kissing his way down my body. He lingers on my stomach, kissing around my belly button, and it tickles so much I let out a low giggle.

"I love your laugh," he says.

"I love you."

Then he looks at me as he drops lower. He nestles his face between my legs and I'm self-conscious at first, letting him touch me there . . . letting his mouth settle. But it feels so good I'm soon lost in it, riding each wave as he brings me closer and closer. . . .

I don't know how much time passes. It's like I'm suspended in air, floating, every feeling better than the last. When I open my eyes I see him, and remember I want us to do this together—I want to take it further.

"Where are the condoms?" I ask.

"In the room."

For once I don't care what happens after, the heartbreak that might follow, the inevitabilities of it all.

We're here now, together.

"Let's go, then," I say.

It's like something has taken over me, and I am moving in a trance. Clothes pulled back on, quick steps out. We're holding hands as we walk back to the inn and climb the rickety stairs, up from the beach, as we sit on the mattress, as we fall into each other again.

The night passes like a dream.

Odie's face just above mine, his lips grazing my cheek as we move together. My hand on his neck, his back, our fingers threading together on the mattress. When it's over he buries his face into my neck, his breaths hot in my ear. And I already want to try it again.

"Are you okay?" he asks.

"I'm better than okay."

"Me too."

He laughs, then I laugh, and we are kissing again.

Nothing else exists except this moment, this room. This bed.

Us.

TWENTY

THE FOURTH WEEK WITH ODIE

When I woke up this morning, I was smiling. I still am as we career out over the water on the sailboat, the wind ripping through my hair. I'm still floating on the memory of it, of the feeling that no matter what happens next, we always have last night.

It was right, perfect even, to lose my virginity to Odie. We love each other, and we want to be with each other . . . it's everything else that's messed up.

"What are you thinking about?" he asks.

"What do you think I'm thinking about?" I raise my eyebrows.

"Me too. So you don't regret it?"

"Of course not," I say. "I'm capable of making my own decisions about my body. I wanted to—I want to again."

"Me too. I guess I just wanted it make sure it was special."

"It was."

Because it was with you, I want to say. Something in me hesitates, though. It's still there, still in the back of my mind—Odie is leaving soon. I have no idea how much time we have left together. It could be weeks . . . or days. . . .

He turns the wheel, cutting over the ocean, the island in our wake. We rented a sailboat out of the Avalon harbor because Odie's racing boat is only for one person. We tried to squish together on it this morning, but it seemed like a bad idea to take it out like that, especially when the sail swings back and forth. There's barely anywhere for me to sit.

This boat is about thirty feet long. It's steady and sure, and the farther we get out onto the water, the more we can see. To our right, herons dive-bomb the surface, pulling up fish.

I point to another spot, just ten yards off, on the other side.

"Over there," I say. "You see?"

There's a pod of dolphins. Their backs and fins visible as they come to the surface for air. The water parts around them, whitecaps crashing over their sides. We can barely keep up.

"This place is perfect," Odie says. "How am I going to leave?"

"I know. It just feels like it's only a matter of time . . ."

I don't say the rest. Since the news broke, we both are feeling it—that whatever fantasy we've been living in, reality will come for us. It's already nipping at our heels. Odie made an anonymous call to the coast guard yesterday, from a phone in town, telling them that he was safe and asking them not to give any resources to searching for him. We're hoping it bought him more time, that maybe once his parents hear he's alive they won't be as panicked. Maybe they'll stop throwing his picture up on the news every five minutes. But everyone on Catalina talks . . . and people have seen him already. Waiters, the rental guy in the harbor, some of the guests at the inn.

How long will it be before someone recognizes him?

Before someone calls a sighting in?

"I'm eighteen now," Odie says. "They can't force me to come home if I don't want to."

"I don't know them, but I get the sense they're used to getting their way."

Odie's quiet, considering it. He moves skillfully around the boat, turning so we're going straight into the wind, then lowering our sail so we can eventually anchor. When I get up to help him he waves me away. I'd normally fight it—growing up on Catalina, you have to know your way around a boat, and it's considered rude to not at least volunteer a hand. But I'm so cozy, sprawled out on the deck, that I'm relieved to just stay where I am.

"I'm not going back because of my dad," Odie says, and I'm not sure if he's talking to me or to himself. "Even when I'm in LA, he never wants to spend time with me. It's not like we ever do anything together. It feels like it's all about control."

"It probably is," I say.

I close my eyes against the sun. It's warming every part of me—the most perfect blanket.

"He just wants me to come back in time to go to Yale," he says. "I'm sure."

"They're not going to give up. You're their kid," I say.

I prop myself up on my elbows, watching as Odie drops anchor. With the rental boat, we were able to get all the way to Emerald Bay—one of the more special places on the island that you can only access by water. Odie looks off at the beach, his eyes unfocused.

"I guess I could call my mom at some point," he says. "Just to tell her I'm okay. It feels like it's going to start this whole thing, though . . . she's going to have to tell my stepdad. Then my dad. Then what?"

"Then I guess you'll deal with them."

"My dad's not easy."

"I know. But what choice do you have? At least if you tell her what's going on, you can try to stay longer . . . you might be able to convince her to give you until the end of the summer."

"She'll let me stay," he says, a certainty in his voice.

"You can't hide forever."

"That's what's weird . . . it doesn't feel like hiding," he says.

"What does it feel like?"

"Like I've been found."

He looks up, then shakes his head. He has on the same blue board shorts he's been wearing nonstop. He bought them at one of the touristy shops along the beach. The top button is open, exposing his stomach muscles. He has a deep tan now from all our time outside, his shoulders even more bronze than the rest of him. Even his hair has gotten longer since he's arrived, the curls more pronounced.

He's so striking like this, it's hard to believe he's mine.

"Things make sense here in a way they haven't in LA," he goes on. "Things with you make sense, Callie."

"This started before me," I say.

Because it did. Everything is mixed up now, for sure, but I don't want to be his escape. His alternate version of reality, the manic pixie dream girl, or the cool girl, or whatever sexist trope I'm supposed to be. I love what we have, but I want it to be its own thing—separate from all the problems he has back home.

Our eyes meet and he comes toward me. As he does, he scans the two other boats in the cove. One of them is an unofficial booze cruise—it's a loud and unruly bunch. A bigger guy with lots of tattoos takes a flying belly flop off the side of the boat, while the couples he's with laugh and laugh. It's not exactly the most romantic scene . . . but everything suddenly seems romantic with Odie watching me.

He stretches out beside me on the deck, using his bicep as a pillow. He has this sweet smile on his face. His brown eyes never leave me.

"What?" I ask.

"I just want more of this. Is that so wrong?"

"It's a little greedy."

"I can't help it."

He inches closer, until his nose is practically nuzzling into my neck.

"I've been thinking . . ." he says.

"Uh-oh . . ."

"What?"

"There's just this mischievous tone in your voice."

He kisses my bare shoulder, then flips up to stare at the sun with me. Immediately I notice it's easier to talk like this—when he's not looking directly at me.

"What are you going to do next year—really," he says. "Are you actually staying to work at the inn?"

"I don't have any other plans. I told you, college isn't an option."

"But you don't have to go to college. You could travel, or—"

"I can't travel," I say. "I need to make money. Then maybe I can see what options I have after that."

"But what if you could travel? Just hear me out . . ."

I let out a long, slow breath, trying my best not to roll my eyes. Odie's world is made up of live-in housekeepers, nannies, trust funds, and Four Seasons vacations. It sucks to always have to remind him we're from different places. That I don't have the same options he does. Most people don't.

"Maybe we could go somewhere. I mean, even if my parents let me change plans, it's going to take a beat to reapply, figure out next steps and all that. Maybe—"

"I can't, Odie," I say. "You know I can't."

"But what if you could?" He says it in a whisper, like I didn't hear him the first time.

"Odie . . . don't make this harder than it is . . ."

Of course I want to travel with him, take a cross-country road trip or backpack around Europe or do whatever teenagers with money do. But there's no way I could afford it. And even if Odie paid, it would mean abandoning my dad and the inn—basically letting the business go under. And if, by some miracle, everything worked out and I could go, would I even like it?

I've barely been off this island.

I've never even left California.

"You never know," he says. "At the very least you have to come visit me."

"Yeah. I guess . . ."

"*Yeah . . . I guess . . .*" He says it in the most unenthusiastic voice possible.

"I don't sound like that."

"You just did. But I forgive you." He leans down and kisses my shoulder again. "You'll see. You can protect your heart if you need to, but you'll see. This is real, Callie."

"I know . . . but . . ."

"You're going to see."

"Okay, then."

"Okay."

Odie rests his hand on my bare stomach, letting his thumb trace circles around my belly button. I'm kind of embarrassed to admit it, but I picked out my bikini this morning with him in mind. Imagining what it might feel like if he untied the strings behind my neck. If he slipped his fingers under the fabric triangles . . . if he tugged it off altogether.

"Weren't you the one who said we should take it in moments?" I whisper.

"I am . . . taking all the moments now. This moment." He moves closer to my ear. "And future ones too. I want them all."

"Greedy."

"I never said I wasn't."

I let his hand roam. First to the edge of my ribs, then down to the top of my bikini bottoms. They're a sparkly purple, glittering in the sun, and when he runs his fingers along the edge I feel crazy turned on.

Maybe I'm feeling greedy too.

"Want to go inside?" he asks. "What's the point of having a cabin if you don't use it?"

"Oh, we should definitely use it."

"Yeah, I don't know why . . . I'm suddenly really tired. I need to lie down."

I give him the biggest, most exaggerated yawn. "Me too—so, so tired."

But when he grabs my hands and helps me up, we're both smiling. We steady each other as we walk on the deck. Each step feels more sure with him there. The booze cruise is yelling and hooting behind us, and we dip down below deck, letting their voices fade.

By the time we get inside and I pull the cabin door shut, his hands are all over me.

TWENTY-ONE

THE FIFTH WEEK WITH ODIE

I'm sitting at a table at the Descanso Beach Club, watching Odie pace up and down the beach. He has my iPhone at his ear. At one point he seems like his eyes are tearing and I wondering what he's saying, but I'm too far away to hear.

"Another Sprite?" The waiter hovers over me, his tray balanced in one hand. He was a senior at my high school when I was a freshman. Jack something . . . He came by the inn at the beginning of the summer to drop off his résumé.

"Sure . . . and some french fries?"

"You got it!" he says cheerfully, scribbling the order on his notepad.

I might be here awhile. Odie finally decided to call his mom, so she would at least know he was alive. He was going to tell her what happened, why he decided to leave, and that he was safe and she shouldn't worry about him. He seemed to think he could convince her to let him stay through the end of the summer, which I found a little unlikely, given the moms I know. They'd all be pissed if their teenager just up and disappeared for weeks on end.

It's weird, though . . . I'm still hoping . . .

I can't help but want more days, more weeks. Just more of him.

The waiter swaps my empty Sprite for a full one, and I start sucking that down, already cruising on my sugar high. Odie turns to make another slow lap on the beach and our eyes meet. He gives me a little wave and smile, like things are going well.

I'm a bit lost without my phone, so I start scanning the bar at the restaurant. Jack the server guy is talking to some girl with long, wavy black hair. It looks like they're flirting, but I can't tell for sure. She glances back, as if she senses me watching them, and I see it's Pita. She does a double take, like she doesn't quite recognize me.

There's an awkward beat, where I'm not sure if she's just going to turn right back around and ignore me. That's what it seemed like would happen based on our last inter-action at the beach. She'd barely make eye contact with me.

But then she says something to the waiter and slowly makes her way over, weaving through the tables.

"Hey, Pita . . ." I say.

Her name feels strange coming out of my mouth—like a word I haven't spoken in too long. There were days when I must've said it twenty times. Maybe more.

"Can I sit?" she says.

"You never have to ask."

"I don't know anymore. . . ."

It's a jab, for sure. But it's not like Pita's been lying around, twiddling her thumbs, missing me all summer. She's been busy too.

"I didn't realize you knew Jack," I say, nodding to the server.

"Jake. We only met last month."

"Cool . . . I mean, he's a good waiter. Really on top of refills."

Pita stares at me over her sunglasses. I can tell she's fighting a smile—that she doesn't want to give me that satisfaction.

"You know I'm leaving for Santa Cruz," she finally says. "In three weeks."

"Three weeks? Seriously?"

"Yeah. We just shipped a bunch of stuff."

Just the thought of it pricks at my eyes. How has the summer already come and gone? What am I going to do without Pita here? Then what will happen when Odie leaves too? It feels like enough heartbreak for a whole year, and it's only August.

"That sucks."

"I thought you'd be relieved."

"Relieved?"

Is she kidding? What does she think of me?

"What? It's not like I've seen you for the last month," she says.

"Pita—I haven't seen you either. You've barely texted me."

I reject this narrative that I'm somehow the bad friend, the one who ditched Pita for a guy. How many times did I try to talk to her about that asshole Brett? She acted like I was blowing everything out of proportion or just being too sensitive. Like I was in my own world, still obsessing about the past and what Harper had done.

Besides, she has Marlowe. Marlowe who has her life together and is going to college and going to study neurobiology, or whatever the hell it is. Marlowe who doesn't have a topless picture of herself floating around the internet. . . .

"I guess I just got sick of everything being all about you," Pita says. "I get the spring was not great for you, but—"

"Understatement," I say.

"Whatever. It was really bad, then, fine. But everything in my life is changing and you're supposed to be my best friend. But it's like . . . you're too consumed with your own stuff to even notice. So yeah, maybe I want to hook up with a guy before college or I want to talk about my roommate at UCSC who seems weird—"

"Her Instagram has a picture of her eating Doritos with her feet. She is definitely weird."

Another almost-smile from Pita—but she resists it. I hate that we're fighting, but I hate it even more that we won't stop fighting. She's leaving so soon and we're still talking about what I did and didn't do this summer. How I failed her.

Doesn't she realize she's failed me too?

Pita looks over my shoulder at Jake or Jack or whoever.

It's like he's totally forgotten about my french fries. Instead he's dropping a bunch of rum punches at a table of retirees. Then he goes back to the server station and waves her over.

"You're dating Jake now?" I ask, unable to hide the annoyance in my voice.

"What does it even matter?" Pita says.

"I don't know . . . it matters to me. You matter to me, Pita."

"Do I?" she asks.

I'm not sure what to say to that, it feels so ridiculous to me. It must take me a beat too long to respond because Pita just lets out a long, low sigh, and stands. Then she goes back to the bar, where she talks to Jake for what feels like forever, then leaves. When she goes she doesn't say goodbye to me. Not even a glance over her shoulder or a wave.

Part of what she's saying is true—the spring was really hard for me. Impossible at times. And she was really there, listening to all my freak-outs and taking my calls in the middle of the night, when I was sobbing so hard I felt like I couldn't breathe. But the whole time all this exciting stuff was happening for her. Everything was falling into place—like where she was going to go to school and what she wanted to study—but if anything, my life had gone in reverse.

For the first time ever, our friendship has been totally out of sync.

I slurp down my second Sprite but it's ages before Jake returns to the table with the fries, which have obviously been sitting under a heat lamp for half the afternoon. He barely says anything, and I wonder if Pita told him who I was (or who I wasn't) to her.

Forget best friends—are we even friends anymore?

"It's going to be okay," a familiar voice calls out.

When I turn, I see Odie bounding up the beach. He comes up on the deck and sits down across from me, in the same seat Pita left free. Then he slides my phone across the table. Before I forget, I open up my calendar and mark down when Pita leaves in three weeks. Whether we're friends or not, it feels like it's the end of an era.

"It's okay?" I ask him, a little skeptical. "Seriously?"

"I mean, it's not *okay* okay," he says. "But my mom understood what happened with my dad. She was really angry . . . but then she understood. She said I can take the ferry back next week but I have to check in with her before that."

"Whoa."

"Child of divorce . . . it has some advantages."

"She's just okay with it?" I ask.

"It's more . . . she assumes it's my dad's fault. She's already annoyed about the whole press conference thing. She said she had a feeling there was more to the story."

I don't know if I should ask, but I can't help myself.

"What about . . . Penelope?"

"My mom didn't know we'd broken up. I guess Pen was hiding it from her parents. It's like she's still so committed to this idea of us. I didn't even tell you . . . she'd gotten this dog, this Pomeranian. She named it Mr. T and kept saying it would be our dog, that it would be ours together. She doesn't even like dogs."

"Where is it now?" I ask.

"I bet when she goes away to college she'll give it to her housekeeper, Evie. Evie is obsessed with dogs," he says. But when he looks up, he must clock my expression. "It sounds serious but it wasn't. At least not for me. We were only together for six months."

There are things that he isn't saying. I feel for Pen, I do, because they lost their virginity to each other. She was probably thinking she and Odie would stay together at college and beyond. And this is where guys can be really dumb—can you blame her for thinking that when they grew up together? When their moms are best friends?

It probably meant everything when they started dating.

"Leaving a trail of heartbreak in your wake, huh?"

I don't look at him as I say it, and he leans down to meet my eyes.

"It's not the same, Callie," he says. "I know it sounds like BS but it's really not the same. First we were just going to prom together . . . then it turned into this whole thing. And I was just going along with it. I don't know. I feel bad, but it wasn't the same."

"Okay . . ."

But how do I know if I can really believe him? Suddenly everything feels all out of whack. Pita and I are barely speaking, and I've just spent weeks with someone who is going to disappear from my life soon. Do I really even know Odie? Why did I think I could trust him? And what's going to happen when Pita leaves next week, before we've even repaired anything?

He bites into a fry, then scrunches his nose, realizing it tastes like cardboard. "I'm sorry I was gone so long."

"I get it."

There must be something in my expression or even the way I say it. It's like he can smell the sadness on me.

"What happened?" he asks. "Are you okay?"

"It's just . . . more stuff with Pita. She was here and . . . what even happened this summer? I feel like I blinked and it's over. You're going to leave soon and . . ."

I barely get out the words before my eyes well. I wipe them with the tips of my fingers, hoping they won't spill over. For a moment I actually convince myself I'm not going to cry.

Before I can explain, Odie is already up, squishing beside me on the chair and pulling me into a hug. He holds me while the tears slip down my cheeks. Then I'm really crying, everything Pita said hitting me at once.

Because Pita's right . . . I have been all about me.

And I don't know what to do now that I've lost my best friend.

TWENTY-TWO

THE SIXTH WEEK WITH ODIE

"You seem better. Happy."

"Buttercream makes everyone happy," I say.

"So does sex," Odie whispers, then gives me a mischievous smile.

"Only good sex," I say, and my face flushes, my whole body reignited.

"I'll take that as a compliment."

I lean in and kiss him—slow, letting my lips linger. They're still tender from this afternoon, which was all a blur. Something clicked in a way it hadn't before, like we aren't in our heads about it, and instead are just moving as one. It's all instinct now, the way we are with each other. Nothing existed outside that room. Every time I'd think I couldn't feel more, or better, Odie would touch me and I'd be lost in him all over again.

Eventually we dragged ourselves out to get food at the

café down the street. Now we're in the inn's kitchen, and he's watching me as I ice cupcakes. Technically it closed hours ago, but Lenora said I could use it to bake tonight. This is my last day off before I have to go back to work tomorrow morning.

I pipe the cream onto the top, moving in a circle. These are molten chocolate cupcakes, but I stuffed them with melted Snickers bars instead of ganache. I crushed the tiniest bit of Snickers into the icing too, just to give the whole thing a cohesive taste. When I'm done with the last one, I put it onto one of the inn's china plates and slide it across the table to him.

"This is so professional," he says. "You've only been baking a year?"

"Since the fall, yeah."

He bites into it, and the tiniest dribble of Snickers melt gets stuck on the corner of his mouth. For a second I think he's going to stop everything to get a napkin but he just takes another bite, and another, downing it before I can even get a word in.

"Good?" I ask.

"Better than good. I'm telling you, you've got to sell these," he says.

Then he picks up another. This time I join him.

We eat together, his mmming the only sound.

Of course I think my desserts are incredible, but I'm also extremely biased. Seeing how much Odie is enjoying them, though, gives me the boost I need. Is it so crazy to think I could do this for a living? That maybe I don't have to go to college, or pursue the same path everyone else is set on? That maybe I can forge something that's all my own?

"When you're deep in thought you get this spaced-out look," Odie says, smirking. He takes a third cupcake, which feels like the ultimate compliment. "Your eyes kind of stare off into the distance."

"Sorry."

"I didn't mean it like that. I was just curious."

"I guess I was thinking about the future." I laugh. "Since meeting you . . . I don't know. It seems different. I can actually picture it. . . ."

"Your dessert truck?"

I smile, just hearing him say it out loud. "Yeah. My dessert truck."

"I can picture my future too. The one I want, not the one everyone else wants for me."

Odie reaches out for me, then runs his fingers down my arm, finally grabbing my hand. We just hold each other like that, both feeling what it feels like to be together in this way. We've touched hundreds of times over the past weeks, but it's this—holding hands—that I will probably miss the most.

"The next few months are going to suck," I say. "I'm already dreading it."

"I know."

"No, you don't know, Odie. You're going to go back to

LA and I'm going to be here still, working at the inn. Without you . . . without Pita. Most of the kids I graduated with are doing something, even if it's just trying out community college."

"I don't want to leave."

"I'm not blaming you."

He looks stricken at just the mention of leaving. His dark eyes follow me as I let go of his hand and drop down to the table, leaning my elbows on it, mirroring him.

"What I was going to say is . . . even if it's going to suck, I wouldn't trade this. I wouldn't change anything. I feel like we were meant to meet."

"Me too," he says. He reaches up and tucks a stray hair behind my ear. "I wouldn't change anything. This has been worth whatever happens to me after. Whatever trouble I get in with my dad. Everything."

We lean in, our foreheads touching. He kisses me again and I close my eyes, losing myself in it. I wish only to stop time now, to slow its passing at the very least.

I want to keep us here, like this, forever.

TWENTY-THREE

THE SEVENTH WEEK WITH ODIE

The lobby is packed this morning. It seems like every guest is either checking in, checking out, or desperately needs something from me—directions, suggestions, reservations, or an understanding nod, as they complain for fifteen minutes about the time it took for Matty to pick them up in the golf cart last night.

"Your bike should be ready at eleven," I say, putting down our landline phone. "The rental place is on Crescent Avenue—it's called Island Adventures. It's right where the ferry gets in. From there you can ride all over the island."

The woman I'm talking to is tall, with a pink bandanna she's turned into a headband. She mentioned she's on a solo vacation to get away from her three young kids.

"Wonderful . . . so amazing," she says, as if she's just grateful to have someone help her. I give her a pamphlet for the bike place. I wrote the confirmation for the rental across the top in Sharpie.

As soon as she's gone, I go back to my favorite hobby: replaying moments with Odie. The nights in room 2, but also the little exchanges we've had. Quick back-and-forths where he said something funny, or the way he put his hand on the small of my back when we were walking in town. He rested it there, his palm warm against my skin.

I'm thinking of those same hands when my phone buzzes with a new text. Part of me hopes it'll be Pita, inviting me to come over before she leaves. Or really anything to indicate she doesn't completely hate me. But instead it's Matty.

MATTY
JUST SAW UR DAD
HE SEEMS PISSED

CALLIE
Y?

MATTY
DUNNO
FYI

Matty is prone to dramatics, so I try not to think too much of it. He and my dad have had their own weird dysfunctional relationship for years, and Matty himself has wondered if he's playing out some unresolved family stuff.

For the most part, I stay out of it.

Another guest approaches, asking for suggestions for which beach to go to. He looks athletic and he says he likes to hike, so I suggest Goat Harbor. I'm passing him the trail map when my dad comes in, his eyes fixed on me the whole time.

"Did you see this?" my dad asks, when the guy breaks off.

He puts the *Catalina Islander* down in front of me. It's the island's local paper, and it comes out every Friday. It's usually filled with stories about the city council meetings or different crimes that were committed on the island. They run ferry schedules and list all the different community events happening that week. I'm not sure why anything would even be relevant to me . . . but then I see Odie's face.

MISSING LOS ANGELES BOY WANTED FOR AS-SAULT ON CATALINA ISLAND

I scan the story, trying to make sense of it. But then I see a few key words: *missing boy, Odysseus Reyes, Brett Wright, assault, witnesses say . . . an exchange over a girl . . .*

There's a small photo at the bottom. At first I don't even connect this Odie to the one I know—he has on a suit and tie, and isn't smiling. His hair is gelled into stiff waves. It's obviously his photo from school, but he seems so serious.

"Did you know about this?" my dad asks.

He rests his finger on the part of the article where it says his full name, then who his parents are, like I'm suddenly having a hard time reading.

"Dad . . . it's not what it looks like . . ." I say.

"What do you mean? He didn't lie to me about who he was and why he was here?" he says, a little too loud. "Now I'm wondering, what exactly wasn't a lie?"

"He had to—"

"*Had to?* This is the person you've chosen to get involved with? Some rich kid who's running away from his life, who didn't even have the decency to tell me who he is?"

Matty was right . . . my dad is beyond pissed. I haven't seen him this way in years. His whole face is pink and I couldn't get a word in even if I wanted to, he's talking so fast. I'm not sure what he knows and what he doesn't so I just wait until he's done.

"Calypso . . . please tell me you are not the girl in this article. Please."

There's nothing I can say. In his mind I've already fucked up royally. Admitting it's me is just more confirmation that I'm a terrible judge of character and shouldn't be trusted to make decisions about my life . . . well, ever.

"I already spoke to the sheriff's office," he says. "If it is you . . . you're going to have to make a statement. This kid's parents want him arrested. They're going to find him, Callie, so if you know where he is then—"

"I don't know where he is."

A lie, but all I can think is I need to protect him. He hit that guy because of me, and I need to at least buy him enough time to get ahead of this—maybe get a lawyer or try to fight it. I don't know how that would work, but I need to at least try to help him.

"You stay here," my dad says.

He taps his finger on the lobby desk, like he means it. Then he goes into his office and shuts the door. When he's gone I just stare at Odie's face in the paper, unable to believe what just happened.

Brett must've seen him in the news. Who knows how many times that press conference played in LA, if it circulated on social media or other outlets. Odie's dad seems powerful enough to have blasted the alert far and wide . . . and now everyone knows where he is. Everyone knows what he's done too.

Matty has reappeared at his post at the front door. He must've been there for a while because his eyes are bugging out, like *See, I told you!* He takes out his phone and covertly texts me, mine buzzing as each one comes in. I don't bother to pick it up, though.

Instead I'm staring at the photo of Odie. He's down at the beach right now, waiting until I get off my shift. There's no way he knows yet—the paper just dropped this morning. It's like all the dreams we had for ourselves, separately and together, are vaporizing with each passing minute. Forget Yale—this could derail his whole life. If he's convicted he'll end up with a criminal record . . . or worse. . . .

What is this going to mean for us?

And for him?

TWENTY-FOUR

THE SEVENTH WEEK WITH ODIE

It's an unbearable wait, but as soon as the lunch shift is over I beg Araceli to cover the desk for me. I need to sneak downstairs and tell Odie what's happening. He needs to know now, and maybe even go back to LA before this all spirals out of control . . . or even more than it has already.

"I'll be back as soon as humanly possible," I say.

"You better . . . I hate it up here." Araceli shifts uncomfortably, unsure what to do.

She took off her apron, so she looks like any other desk attendant in her Ogygia Inn polo. I give her more promises as I push past Matty and go around the side of the hotel, picking up the stairs that hug the building.

"What happened?" he calls after me. "What did he say?"

"Don't worry about it. You didn't see me leave, okay?"

I'm walking as I'm talking to him, and I glance back to check that the curtains in our apartment are closed. I wait until Matty nods, just making sure he understands that I'm serious, then I disappear down the stairs.

My dad was in his office for a long time. I heard him talking on the phone but I couldn't make out a word. At a certain point he slipped out the back exit without even saying goodbye. I know he's furious with me, that in his mind this is just another bad decision, another dubious guy I've let trick me into thinking I'm in love. But I can't consider that right now.

All I can think about is Odie.

The story is spreading fast—too fast. Because of who Odie's dad is, there are already reels and TikToks about Salvador Reyes's son and how he disappeared while out on his boat. Now they've all been updated, people following the story closely to speculate about what he did to this poor kid on Catalina Island. There hasn't been a single account that's painted him in a positive light. Some are saying he's a spoiled trust fund brat, wasting everyone's time and energy . . . others are saying he's a brute and a monster.

I'm worried for him, but my panic has been growing with each reel I've watched and every Reddit thread I've gone down. Now I'm even more worried for myself. People online are mining all Odie's old posts on social media and trying to figure out who the girl referenced is. It's only a matter of time before one of Brett's friends says something or releases my name. What happens if that old photo of me surfaces? What are people going to say? What are his parents going to think of me after this?

Any chance we had at a real relationship is slipping away. . . .

What couple could survive this?

When I get to the third-floor landing I check the beach. I can just see the sliver of shore where he usually hangs out when he's not sailing. He's not there, but the dinghy still is—I can just barely see it beyond the bend. I keep going, about to try the room instead, thinking he must be sleeping or reading—he ended up buying himself a graphic novel last night when we were in town. But as I get closer I see the door is open.

Inside, I hear my father's voice. Then Odie's.

My hands are shaking as I start down the last few steps, thinking of what will happen now that we've been discovered. This room—our sweet room where we shared so many important moments—is not ours anymore. And the sound of my father's voice is a reminder it never was.

"You have our sincerest apologies," a woman says. "Truly."

When I get to the door it's a horrific sight. Odie stands beside the bed with his dry bag at his feet. It's stuffed to the brim. The rest of the room isn't the same place it was even this morning—the mattress is stripped, with the sheets and blankets folded on top of it. All the camping gear and supplies I brought down for him are in a cardboard box on the table. Even the romance novel is back on its spot on the shelf.

It's like Odie was never here at all.

The woman is short and immaculately dressed in a beige linen pantsuit. Her hair is dyed a dark red, almost burgundy color. It looks like she's had an expensive blowout—every wave and curl is perfectly in place. An oversized pink Hermès bag sits on one shoulder. I don't know a lot about designer bags, but I know that thing costs thousands of dollars, maybe more.

"What's going on?" I ask, and they all turn to look.

I'm too hesitant to even acknowledge Odie in front of my dad, but he runs to me and throws his arms around my shoulders, pulling me close. It's a desperate, grasping hug. The intensity of it scares me.

Is this the end? How could it be ending now, so soon?

I was sure we had more time.

"Okay, that's enough," the woman says.

She comes over and taps Odie on the shoulder with her perfectly manicured hand. At first I thought it was his mom, but I remember his mom from the clips of the press conference and this woman seems nothing like that . . . She's stern and looks much younger than I'd expect. She's at most twenty-eight? Thirty?

"This is Nina," Odie says, as if reading my mind. "My dad's girlfriend."

Odie mentioned his parents split because his dad had cheated on his mom with his twentysomething assistant, and now he has this pseudo stepmom who isn't that much older than him. I'd pictured Nina differently, though, more like a free-spirited type.

"We were just leaving," she says.

"See?" Odie whispers, still holding my arm. "My dad cares so much he didn't even bother to come himself. He sent Nina to get me."

"He's closing a deal, Odysseus," Nina says. "He's spent every second of the past few weeks worried about you—he's entitled to one day of normalcy."

"Whatever, Nina," Odie says.

"You can't just leave," I say, looking from him to Nina. "His mom said—"

"His mother should've never said anything. The fact that she knew you were here for days without sharing that with us . . . I can't even."

Nina pushes past me, her Manolo Blahniks clicking against the wooden stairs. She flinches as she goes through the doorway, pulling her shoulders in as though she's afraid to touch anything.

"Now, Odysseus," she calls over her shoulder. "We have to get you back to Los Angeles. The helicopter is waiting for us. We have an emergency call with Lev tonight."

"Lev?" I ask him.

"Our lawyer," Odie says, hoisting his dry bag over his shoulder. "She flew here to get me."

The more he packs up, the closer he gets to the door . . . the more the panic swells inside my chest. This can't be goodbye. It wasn't supposed to go like this, with him getting dragged off the island. I thought we'd at least have one more night.

"Maybe Callie can come with us," Odie says, looking down at Nina.

"Absolutely not," my father says.

Nina doesn't even turn back in response.

"Please," she says, her voice full of disgust. "None of this would've happened if it wasn't for her. We know all about Calypso."

We know all about Calypso.

What does she mean by that? Did they somehow find out about the photo, or the exchange I had with Brett? The fight I had with him before we even ran into him that night? I want to defend myself, tell her that Brett said heinous things to me, that he was totally out of line and Odie stepped in . . . but somehow all of it feels irrelevant now. She doesn't know me, and she definitely doesn't care.

She doesn't even acknowledge me—just climbs the rest of the stairs to the lobby. Odie hugs me once more, kissing me on the cheek in a way that makes me wonder if this is the last time. Will we ever see each other again? How will he even get in touch with me?

It's not like we text . . . or he even knows my number. . . .

"It's not goodbye, I promise," he whispers in my ear.

But it feels that way. I don't even care that my father is watching us. I grab him and pull him close again . . . for one last moment. I can't help but be greedy now.

I feel his breath on my neck, his strong arms holding me. *I don't want you to go*, I say with my body, my hands on his back, nuzzling my face into his chest. *You can't leave me here. Not now. Not like this.*

"Odysseus!" Nina's voice calls down to him.

He finally pulls away, and I can see now he's tearing up too. He mouths *I'm sorry* before heading up the stairs, his pack slung over his shoulder. All I can do is watch him . . . he's leaving whether I want him to or not.

As much as I knew this was going to happen, some way, at some point, it still feels surprising. And I can't help but want it to be different, to wish it hadn't happened *this* way. Was there any way we could've prevented this? How did I not see this coming?

"I am so disappointed in you, Calypso," my dad says from somewhere behind me.

When I spin around he has his arms crossed over his chest, his jaw set in a way where I can see the bone. Of course I know it was wrong to let Odie stay here, to hide him in the inn, but it wasn't a choice, really. He needed me. And in ways I'm only starting to understand, I needed him too.

"You lied," my dad says. "You were keeping him down here, in a room we've had closed for over a year. I'm not even going to get into the liability issues on that—if anything had happened, his family could've sued us to oblivion. No, I can't even think of that."

"You told them. You called and told them where he was," I say, putting it together.

"I had to. You didn't give me a choice."

"You could've talked to me about it—there's always a choice," I say, and the tears are coming fast now, the whole room fuzzy.

"You're not thinking about anyone but yourself lately," he says. "Now everyone has to suffer because of your bad judgment. This isn't the child I raised. I can't even imagine what your mother would say."

It hurts more than I would've thought it would. Just the mention of her and all the breath leaves my body. I'm silent, waiting for him to see how much it stung. Waiting for him to take it back, to say he didn't mean it that way.

But instead he just shakes his head and points to the box of camping gear. "Take this upstairs, will you. And lock up when you're done. I don't want anyone knowing this happened. If even one guest had seen someone in here . . . It's bad enough we have a boarded-up room on the property."

He walks past me and leaves, letting out an angry sigh, like it physically hurts him to have to deal with this. I'm frozen in that spot long after he goes, trying to process what just happened. This room—the room where Odie went from a stranger to so much more, where I lost my virginity and we spent countless hours cuddling and laughing, just being together—it's empty now. I can feel that emptiness in my bones, even as I try to tell myself that I'll see him again, that this isn't where our story ends. . . .

It all feels hollow, though, and none of it makes me feel better. Odie is gone and I'm still here. He's not coming back, no matter how much I want him to. Our lives collided for this one brief summer—that was all—and now I'm stuck on this island without him.

TWENTY-FIVE

THE FIRST WEEK WITHOUT ODIE

"I ordered tacos from the Sand Trap." My dad's voice is on the other side of the door. He knocks once, as if that might help. "Callie? Did you hear me?"

He tries the handle, but I already knew he would, so it's locked.

It's been locked a lot lately.

"I'm good," I call out from under the covers.

"I'll leave them on the table for you," he says. I can see from the inch under the door that he's waiting there, the shadow of his feet moving ever so slightly. "Callie? I'm sorry . . . about everything."

I don't respond. He shifts, the shadow moving again. It takes a beat before he finally goes away.

"Too late," I say, and even the words make my eyes well.

I return to my phone. It's paused on *Fated Loves*, this cheesy reality show I've been bingeing. There are ten seasons so far, and I'd never watched any of them, so now whenever I'm not working that's what I do. Just disappear into it for a while . . . rooting for Bianca or Lionel or even Joshua, the sexy bartender (who's not supposed to date any of them, but it seems like maybe he doesn't play by the rules). It makes me feel better somehow, thinking that even the dumbest people are finding love. That they're kissing and hooking up and the world is still turning . . . even if it isn't for me.

It's been four days since Odie left. He immediately found me on Instagram and I gave him my number, but it somehow makes it harder that he's been texting me. It's like we're still together . . . but we're not. There's no future for us, no chance that he'll be back anytime soon, or that I'll be visiting him in LA. He hasn't said it outright, but I get the sense I'll never be allowed in either his mom's or his dad's house—that they both blame me for everything that's happened on the island. I'm an easy scapegoat, and the little they've been able to find out about me online isn't good.

Since the news broke about Brett pressing charges, Odie's parents made him alert Yale, and they withdrew his acceptance. Odie was okay with it, considering he didn't really want to go there in the first place, but now he's stuck in limbo for the next few months until they figure out if Brett will settle out of court. I'm not even completely sure how it would work, but Odie's parents are basically throwing as much money as they can at the problem in the hopes it'll go away.

I shouldn't, but I go back to my thread with him. There

are three texts that I still haven't answered. He sent them hours ago and I still can't bring myself to respond.

Of course it isn't my fault. That much I've realized more with each passing day. But the internet—and Odie's parents—have decided otherwise. Online the story keeps morphing, becoming this distorted thing I don't even recognize anymore. Different social media accounts are latching on to different details, others following new threads they think could be relevant. It has all the makings of a true-crime saga, except no one was murdered. As far as I can tell, Brett didn't even get a black eye.

I was online yesterday when I saw it for the first time in months: my photo—*the* photo—was up on TikTok. They'd put one of those black squares over my boob. The person said something about me seducing Odie and holding him on the island against his will. I watched it twice before I just snapped and turned my phone off.

My dad must've heard rumors that the photo reemerged, because everything about his tone has shifted. He's been almost apologetic that he called Odie's parents. And he definitely feels terrible that we were ever fighting at all. When I went and gave my statement to the Catalina sheriff, he waited outside the whole time. Then afterward he kept saying he was proud of me and that this was a really hard situation.

Hard situation . . .

That felt like the understatement of the year.

I go back to *Fated Loves*. Bianca is choosing between Thomas and Minnie in terms of who she wants to move on to the next round with. The audience knows they've all taken compatibility tests and she's only truly meant for one of them, though we don't know who. I'm partially thinking it's Minnie, just because they're both more introverted than the other contestants and—

My phone lets out a low ping. The little alert bar comes up at the top of the screen. It's a reminder for a calendar event. PITA LEAVES FOR COLLEGE. It's happening in one day.

I'd forgotten I put it in three weeks ago. It seems stupid now, because I'm sure Pita heard at least parts of what happened with Odie and she never even bothered to reach out. She hasn't texted or called or given me any reminder that she's leaving tomorrow. It's like that fight we had at the beach club was our last conversation, and she's totally okay with that.

Annoyed, I go back to Bianca. She's on a date with Thomas to try to figure out how she really feels about him. They're in this bar talking and he's touching her leg. Now she's sitting on a white couch and she's narrating that it actually gave her the ick. After a while I pause it, unable to concentrate.

How could Pita just leave before we make up?

Is she really going to go without saying goodbye?

No matter how bad things have gotten between us, we've always found our way back to each other. This is the longest we've gone without hanging out or at least texting, and it hurts to think another four months might slip away before she comes home for Christmas break. By then . . . what will we even have to say to each other? Is this how friendships end?

I click off *Fated Loves* and get out of bed. I've been in the same T-shirt and boxers for almost two days now, and my hair is a mess, the back all tangled in knots. I brush out as much as I can and change into clean clothes, then splash cold water on my face.

It's the first time I've showed any kind of motivation since Odie left. It feels right, though, that if I'm going to try for anything, I should try to see Pita one last time.

I grab my tote bag and head out the door.

Pita grew up in a narrow three-bedroom bungalow on Sumner. Her mother painted it bright turquoise a few years back and it's still the most cheerful house on the block, the walkway lined with potted roses. Tiny stained-glass artworks hang in the living room window—sunset vistas, a mountaintop, even a little one that looks like their dog Rue.

I get there just after dinner but the kitchen is dark. There's none of the usual sounds—plates and pots clinking together in the sink, the screech of the oven door as her mom pulls out a tray of simmering pork, or Pita shouting to her brothers. Their bicycles aren't even in their usual spot, all five lying against the brick wall.

I knock once, twice. From the front steps I can see into the living room. The curtains are drawn and only one light is on. The television is off, though, and no one is on the couch. I pull out my phone and text her.

CALLIE

I'M AT UR HOUSE

I CAME TO SAY GOODBYE

AND SORRY

It seems like not enough somehow, just that word—*sorry*. I want to tell her I'm sad we were fighting this summer, the most important summer, our last one before everything changes for good. That maybe she was right . . . I've been so wrapped up in my own stuff this year. Things were hard but I could've been there for her more and thought more about what she was going through. The truth is, every time she talked about college or leaving, it made me so sad I just wanted to change the subject. It felt like some awful confirmation that we were losing each other, that in months we wouldn't have anything in common.

Pita would be a college freshman, going to frat parties and choosing a major.

And I would be the same person I've always been . . . a desk attendant at the Ogygia Inn.

More thoughts come, even as I try to push them away. I'm the one who couldn't get her act together to write her admission essays and turn in her applications. The one who took the topless selfie that wouldn't die. I'm the one who got the guy she loved into a fight—the only fight he's ever been in—and now he's been charged with assault.

Of course I was having a hard time being happy for Pita . . . it's like she's made all the right choices and I've made all the wrong ones. And now her life is speeding ahead and I'll never be able to catch up. Everyone says it's not a race, that it's not a competition, but then why do I keep feeling left behind?

I drop down to the steps, resting my back against the front door. When I check my phone, Pita still hasn't responded. It's possible they're at dinner. Her parents have always loved Antonio's, this pizza spot only locals go to. We went there with my dad after graduation.

I wait . . . and wait. At some point Dolores, the eighty-year-old woman who lives next door, notices me as she's making tea. She peeks out her curtains a few times to see if I'm still there.

"They left this morning," she finally calls out. "They're taking Lupita to school."

"I thought that . . ." I say, my throat tight.

Dolores takes a sip of her tea, then shakes her head. "Do you need something?"

How do I even answer that question?

Instead I just thank her and head off down the street. I consider leaving Pita some long rambling voice note, like a crazed ex-boyfriend, explaining how sorry I am and how I wanted to come tell her in person. But it seems unfair to do that now, when she's probably just getting to her new dorm and exploring the campus for the first time. I don't want to sap even another ounce of joy from that.

But as the sky darkens, it feels heavy, impossible even, to know I ruined our friendship. It was bad enough, how I acted this past year, but then I lost myself in the summer. In long, meandering days with Odie, in dreaming about the future we could have, all the possibilities. The whole time I ignored the person who meant the most to me.

And for what? What am I left with?

What do I do now?

TWENTY-SIX

The kitchen is quiet. All the other staff have left and it's just Lenora and me, moving around each other as we plate the last two lunches. She puts a big scoop of garlic mashed potatoes down and layers the roast chicken on top. I plate the turkey club and then hit the bell to let Araceli know they're ready.

"You already seem a little better, just doing things," Lenora says, after Araceli retrieves the plates. "Apparently small accomplishments can help with depression."

"Who said I'm depressed?" I ask, filling the dirty pot with water.

"Callie . . ."

Lenora turns the oven knob off. She gives me this look like, *don't lie to me.* So I don't—instead I put all my attention on the pot, scrubbing at the burnt goo in the bottom.

"I mean . . . everyone I went to high school with has left," I say. "My best friend left, even though we're basically not friends anymore. And the guy I fell in love with this summer left and is now in a lot of trouble because of me, and his parents think it's all my fault, and a really awful selfie I took of myself resurfaced. . . ."

"It's actually a beautiful picture of you, Callie," Lenora says. "And he's not in trouble because of you—he's in trouble because of *him*. You didn't tell him to hit someone."

"True."

"You're being too hard on yourself."

"Yeah, I guess I am a little depressed."

I don't mention the other, more depressing development. It's nearly October. Most tourists have left the island and business has slowed, which always puts my dad in a foul mood. As much as he's trying to be more conscientious around me, I can feel his stress in every interaction. He's started using coupons at all our local places, and sometimes just orders dinner for me, saying he can go without.

This season was supposed to be a turning point for us . . . but it feels like things are only getting worse. He's even talking about laying off some of the cleaning staff and having me pitch in more and have Matty take on some of the maintenance stuff. I used to like the fall, when the island returned to us locals, but now I just associate it with stress and worry.

I keep wondering if the inn will survive.

"If you and Odie are meant to be, it'll work out, Callie," Lenora says.

"Everyone says that. Or you and my dad."

"Because it's true. No one thought your parents had a chance, and they were crazy in love. But eventually it all came together for them."

I set the pot in the drying rack, then go to work on the greasy sheet pans. I don't even bring up Pita again, because there's no way for Lenora to make me feel better. We ended up having a long text exchange two weeks after she left. I apologized for everything that happened and said she was right, I had been wrapped up in all my own problems. We agreed we'd hang out over Thanksgiving break and I should come visit her at Santa Cruz in the spring, once she was more settled. But it's not like we've talked much beyond that. And even when we do talk, it isn't the same, easy dynamic it used to be.

No joking, no mentions of random stuff.

I keep hoping the same thing I do for Odie—that if it's meant to work out, we'll come together again. Sometimes friendships go through ups and downs. Maybe we're just weathering our first true hard season.

"I'm going to head to the market," Lenora says, grabbing the grocery bag. "Are you okay finishing up? When I get back you can help me prep dessert tonight. I was thinking mango mousse. Maybe fresh whipped cream . . ."

"Sure . . . why not?"

"When you say it like that, it sounds like you have nothing better to do. But I guess I'll take it. Help is help."

"I would love to!" I say dramatically, then put a soapy hand over my heart.

Lenora sticks her claw clip in her mouth while she pulls her hair back, tucking in a few stray strands. She smiles when she's done, then kisses me on the cheek before heading out.

There aren't many guests, which means there aren't many dishes, so I finish them quickly. Afterward I go back out to the front desk and organize the extra toiletries, then straighten out all the different tour pamphlets. I set aside the ones for rental places that aren't open in the winter. There might be something to what Lenora said about accomplishing things, because after I make a dinner reservation for some guests I actually do feel better.

Just the tiniest bit.

"Excuse me," a man says as he slips past Matty at the front door. "Are you Calypso?"

I'm not wild about that question. Last month we had a few people come in, high off some stupid TikTok reel, looking to take a picture with me. I was even stopped in town on my way to pick up eggs for Lenora. But this guy is my dad's age. He's wearing a navy polo shirt with embroidery on it. When I look closer I see it says *Island Vessel Exchange*, and I realize I have seen him before, down at one of the storefronts near the harbor.

"Who's asking?" I say, just to be careful.

"I'm here to pick up a Bieker Moth. Salvador Reyes sent me, says it's down in the cove here?" He's a big guy, with large, meaty hands. He rests them on the front desk as he waits, his fingers rapping against the wood.

Odie and I have been texting less and less. In truth, it's easier for me when we aren't talking, because I can just be here, in my own world, without wishing I was in his. But he did mention they might pick up the boat soon . . . I just didn't realize how soon. Now that it's fixed, we anchored it just a few yards off the coast. It's been there for over a month now. As silly as it sounds, I've liked staring out the window and seeing it in the water. Watching it drift in the breeze. Sometimes I find myself wandering the beach, stopping in to just sit by it or spread my towel out on the rocks nearby. It's like Odie and I are still connected somehow, like it's this thread tethering me and him.

"Didn't see it in the parking lot, and I . . ." the man continues. He spins around, trying to figure out what he's missing.

"You have to go down the stairs on the other side of the deck," I say. "It's out back, off Pebbly Beach Road. You'll see it a few yards out. I can show you."

I don't want to, but I do. The man follows me out the lobby doors and down to the side stairs—the ones I took dozens of times every day when Odie was staying here. I point him to the boat, then suggest he bring it around to the other side of the beach, by Lover's Cove, where there's a ramp. It's light enough he should be able to drag it up and load it into his truck.

He thanks me and disappears down the steps.

"He's picking up the boat?" Matty asks when I come back inside.

"I guess."

"You didn't know?"

The way he says it, it sounds like an accusation, like what does it mean that Odie didn't tell me? What does it mean that I didn't know it was happening today, of all days? Matty has been especially protective of me these past weeks. Constantly reminding me it's okay, that he has my back, and even inviting me to hang out with him and his little sister, who was a few years above me in high school. I know he's just trying to be nice, but it feels a little condescending. Apparently it's obvious, how sad I am. Everyone can tell just by looking at me.

"I didn't know when, but I knew," I say.

Then I go back to my post at the front desk. Part of me wants to text Odie to just say the guy is hauling off his boat, but it's only going to prolong things between us. The chances of us being together are infinitely small, and I'm trying to force myself to accept that, despite Lenora's platitudes. I can't keep getting pulled back into the fantasy of what it could've been or what it might be still.

I have to move on.

Let him go, whether I want to or not.

Through the patio windows, I can see the guy in the water, sailing the boat around the other side of the beach until it's out of sight. It's strange to watch it go—the only proof that Odie was really here, that we were really together. It wasn't until he was gone that I realized we hadn't taken a single photo together.

I'm checking the inn's upcoming bookings—my new nervous habit—when the guy comes back through the lobby a little while later. His truck is idling outside, just beyond the lobby entrance, in the parking lot. His hands and shirt are dirty from hauling the boat up. I think maybe he wants to use our restroom, or he's about to ask for a glass of water, but then he pulls something from his back pocket.

"All set." He hands me a white envelope that's been neatly folded in half. It has my full name on it in block letters. "That should settle it. Thanks again."

Before he explains any further, he turns, heading back to his truck. I'm not exactly sure what to expect when I open the envelope. The cashier's check inside has my name printed on it. Then I see the amount . . . thirty thousand dollars.

It feels like a sick joke. Why would this guy pay me out for the boat? Does he expect that I'm going to pass this along to Odie's dad? Or is it some kind of weird test to see if I'm honest enough to return the money?

I can't think of any good reason why he'd do this.

It makes no sense.

After a long while, I take out my phone. Before I can overthink it, I'm dialing Odie's number, listening to the sound of each ring.

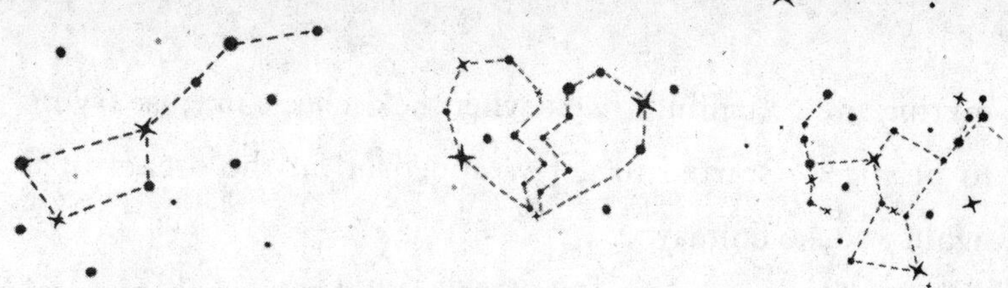

TWENTY-SEVEN

"Callie?"

His voice brings me back—to that room, to my head on his chest, to those long meandering days when time seemed irrelevant. I don't want to love him anymore, but as soon as I hear him say my name, I know I still do.

Maybe I always will.

"Odie . . . hi . . ."

There's a silence on the other end, and I gesture to Matty at the front entrance of the inn, signaling he should watch the desk. The office has been open since this afternoon, when my dad left. I push inside and close the door behind me.

"I kind of thought . . . after our last text . . ." he says.

I immediately know what he means. When he reached out weeks ago, I told him it was too hard to still talk to him. That I needed space to move on from everything that had happened, and it was impossible when he was constantly texting me or calling. Even when he'd check in, just trying to be nice, I started to get wrapped up in the dream of it again . . . the fantasy. . . .

Would we end up together? What did it mean that he was calling me now?

Was he talking to Penelope still? Would he meet someone else?

Would I be replaced?

I remind myself that nothing has changed—that I'm not calling to reconnect or tell him I'm coming to Los Angeles soon for a visit. This call has one purpose and one purpose only.

"I just wanted to tell you that the guy from Island Vessel Exchange showed up here today. He hauled off the boat—your boat."

"Oh . . ."

"And he gave me a check. Do you know anything about that?"

Again, there's a long pause. I sit down in my dad's office chair, waiting it out. The big wooden desk is covered with opened mail and papers. He still has a framed photo of me and my mom from when I was a toddler. We're walking on the beach, holding hands.

"What is this?" I ask, when he doesn't say anything. "Is it some creepy hush money? I don't want this, I never asked for—"

"No, Callie. No. Definitely not," he says.

"Then what is it? Why would you do that?"

He lets out a low breath. "I didn't do it . . . my dad did."

"Your dad doesn't even like me. In fact, I'm pretty sure he hates me. It seems like both your parents think this is all my fault, that I'm somehow responsible for all of this."

"No—it's not like that, Callie."

"Then what's it like?" I ask.

It's humiliating, and it hits me now, all at once. Not only do they think I'm the one who got Odie into the fight that caused Yale to rescind his acceptance, but they also think I'm stupid enough to take money from them. They probably think I'll have to testify at a trial or something, so they need to bring me onto their side. I'm not doing it—I'm not agreeing to this deal without even knowing what it is. I don't want any part of this.

"I told them what happened."

"What do you mean?"

"I told them how we met," he says. "Or really . . . why we met."

I think back to that night, to the rain that was coming at me sideways. The sting of it against my face and arms as I dove under the surface, looking for him again and again.

"You saved my life, Callie," he finally says. "And you might not want to talk to me anymore and we might not ever be together, but I'm grateful. And once I told them . . . they were grateful too."

"I did what any decent person would do."

"No . . . most people wouldn't do that."

I sink lower in the chair, unsure if that's true. It seemed so obvious to me. There was no way I wasn't going to at least try to pull him out of the water. And maybe it was reckless, to think I was a strong enough swimmer that I'd make it. That I'd succeed.

"I know how much our relationship cost you," Odie says. "Everything with Pita. And how the photo came back up . . . it just all sucks."

"It cost you too."

"Did it? I never really wanted to go to Yale in the first place."

"No, the charges. Brett."

Odie lets out another breath. I wonder where he is, if he's in his bedroom, if he's at his mom's or his dad's. That first time he ever tried me he'd FaceTimed, and then he'd showed me the things in his mom's house. The posters and photos in his bedroom. The surfboards piled in his walk-in closet.

"I'd do it again," he finally says.

"I feel the same way. I'd do everything the same way too."

It's sweet somehow, agreeing on it, but where does that leave us? And why does it matter when we're still in the same place? When we're still miles apart, with no chance of ever going to the same college or the same parties or seeing each other again?

"I said if they were going to sell the boat the money

should go to you," he says. "That you deserved something for helping me—I was no one to you."

"If this means I have to testify or . . ."

"It doesn't mean that. I don't even know what will happen with that. Because Brett technically threw that beer on you first, they might toss the case out entirely. A few of the people in the ice cream shop came forward as witnesses."

"I don't know . . . still . . ."

"Look, they don't approve of us, but my mom still says how she can't believe you did that. How lucky she is that you saved me . . . that that's all that matters. You should take it, Callie."

Thirty thousand dollars is a lot of money. Too much money. It's hard not to start dreaming of what I could do with it, if it might be the help we need to save the inn.

"No strings?" I ask.

"No strings."

"I'm glad I called."

"I am too. But not because of that."

Just end the call. Say thank you and goodbye, I think. Every minute we're on the phone together is dangerous, and I don't want to hear how his parents are grateful to me. I don't want to think of him lying in his room, alone, with only an ocean between us. We're from two completely different worlds and we should keep it that way.

We need to keep it that way.

"I should go," I say. "Thank them from me. It means something, it really does."

"Callie?"

Hang up, I think. *Pretend you didn't hear.* But I stay there, with the phone pressed to my ear, waiting for him to say what he always says at the end of every call. At the end of every text exchange, when I'm certain this will never work and we will never see each other again.

"I love you. And you don't have to say it back, but I do. And I can't promise I won't randomly text you to say that or I won't send you random stuff in the mail with a card that says that. I don't know that I'll ever stop. It feels like I can't."

"You will," I say, but my throat tightens, and I'm not sure I actually believe it.

We both need to move on, though, to go our separate ways and live our separate lives. I can't hold out hope that circumstances will change and we'll suddenly be right for each other. That the timing and everything else will work out in our favor.

"I don't think I can," he says, quieter this time.

"I have to go, Odie. I'm sorry."

Then I do manage to hang up, letting the silence fill the small office. I delete his number from my phone and decide I'm not going to answer if he calls again. He can do whatever he wants . . . I just won't let it affect me anymore.

We had so many happy days together.

And now it's time to let go.

EPILOGUE

"You sure you're good?" Pita asks, moving around me in the cramped kitchen. "I could stay if you need help. It looks like they're going to break through the window any second."

She peers out the front of the truck, making uncomfortable eye contact with a group of teens. I open at five, but people have started showing up around four thirty. The line is already wrapped around the corner.

"They always look like that," I say. "Sugar is an addictive substance."

"For real."

"But no—you go," I say, organizing the cupcake boxes. "This is your first Friday night in town. I want you to have fun. Go find your friends."

Pita brought down two of her friends from UCSC—her roommate, Anna, and this guy Zeb they're both close to. I've hung out with them enough now, over the past ten months or so, that it feels like I'm genuinely friends with them too. Sometimes Zeb will even text me *LAist* or *Eater* articles I've been featured in.

They're wandering around Abbot Kinney somewhere, probably browsing the clothing stores or crystal shops that line the main drag. Out of all the events I work, the First Fridays in Venice is one of my favorites, because it's so lively. There are bands and street performers. By the end of the night it all feels like one big party.

"If you insist," Pita says. "If these people start ransacking the truck I'll come back."

"You better."

I hug her tight before she leaves, grateful she's here. In my new city, in my new food truck, visiting me for the first time. There were days last fall when I wasn't completely sure how things would end up with us, or if our friendship was permanently damaged by the summer. But once I visited her at school in February, things got easier. Maybe it also got easier because I was suddenly moving forward in my own life. Pursuing something I actually cared about.

The cupcakes are all lined up in the fridge, and I have all the cookies bagged already—I'm selling them as singles, and by the half dozen. The Crushed-branded napkins and forks are stacked next to the window so they're easy to grab and throw in as I go. I take a deep breath, trying to organize my brain before the onslaught, then I raise the red shade and open the front window.

"Ready? Let's crush this!" I call out, and everyone in line cheers.

I never meant for it to be my unofficial slogan, but I did it once and now everyone kind of expects it.

The first hour goes by in a blur. Most people are buying stuffed cupcakes for themselves and at least a few friends, though I have limits on how much one person can take. I'm supposed to be at First Fridays from five to nine, but I always sell out by seven thirty. I try to cap the line when I know I'm running low on inventory, so people don't hate me. Last month I had to give out vouchers to five customers who were furious when they waited for a half hour and ended up with nothing.

It wasn't always like this, though. Things have been moving really fast—in a good way. I immediately told my dad about the check Odie's parents had given me, and how I wanted to put the money toward saving the inn. That's when I found out my dad had made his own decision about the Ogygia's future. He'd looked at the recent offers from developers and realized he'd been fighting so hard for something he didn't even enjoy anymore. He was always stressed, and to do a massive renovation like the one the hotel needed, he'd have to take out a third mortgage. In the end, it wasn't worth it.

He finally sold the place in January and was able to pay off all our debts. Afterward, he even had enough to buy a condo on the island, right by the pet cemetery (which sounds creepy but we've always loved it), and give everyone who worked there generous severance packages. I knew he'd been under so much pressure, trying to hold it all together, but it wasn't until I actually saw my dad in retirement that I realized how much happier he is. He's been fishing. And snorkeling again. He's started talking photos of the bison on the island, using my mom's vintage cameras.

Once I was absolutely certain there were no strings attached to the check, I decided to save some of the money and invest the rest in a pop-up dessert cart based in Avalon. As soon as the busy season hit, I set up every Thursday, Friday, and Saturday night on the corner of Crescent and Catalina Avenue, serving my stuffed cupcakes and crushed candy cookies. Within the first two weeks I started selling out within an hour, and I had to rent a commercial kitchen space to keep growing. I took everything I made and reinvested it in a used food truck in Los Angeles. I just opened in September.

Tapping into the boat money again, last month I rented a little house in El Sereno, this quiet neighborhood that's close to downtown and Highland Park. I have a spot to park the truck when I'm not working, and the rent is affordable compared to the rest of the city. It's not fancy, but I finally feel like things are falling into place for me. That I don't have to justify not going to college or not pursuing all the things my friends from high school did. I have something I'm passionate about, and I'm making money . . . this is just more *me*.

Not taking on student loans is a bonus.

"Can I take a selfie with you?" the girl in the front of the line asks. She already has her phone out and she's pulling up her camera.

The question still makes me nervous. So far, Crushed Confections has been written up by everyone from the *LA Times* to *Time Out*, and then all these websites where they tell you exactly where a food truck is at any given moment in time. I don't love getting my picture taken, but a few of the outlets have posted me serving from the window. Things have been quiet for so long . . . I just worry someone will make the connection that I'm the Callie who had that whole unfortunate selfie situation. Who went viral on TikTok for her connection to Salvador Reyes's kid.

"I don't love photos, but . . ." I smile as she clicks a few shots.

"Oh, thank you, thank you," she says after she examines the photo. "It's perfect."

She takes her half dozen sugar swirl cookies and her berry blast cupcake. I have to remind myself that I'm not the girl from the topless selfie anymore. That was never me, no matter how much those guys tried to convince me it was.

I'm Callie Quinn. Daughter, friend . . . now a small-business owner. Even those titles can't really encapsulate a person. They can only try.

When I realize I'm down to my last thirty cupcakes, I take a pause at the register and bring out my stanchion sign that reads SOLD OUT. I carry it to the very back of the line, behind a couple who've been waiting for at least a half hour. I'm turning to go back when I hear a familiar voice.

"Don't tell me I'm too late," he says. "I was sitting in rush hour traffic. I had to see the number one dessert truck in LA myself."

Odie is walking toward me—or really, jogging toward me. He has on a white linen button-down and navy shorts. His hair is different than it was last summer. It's cropped close to his head, just a little longer on top. He seems nervous when we lock eyes, but then he smiles.

It's automatic, how I smile back.

I want to run to him, to hug him, but I don't think I'm entitled to that anymore. Too much time has passed. There've been too many texts I didn't respond to, too many times I told him I needed to move on.

So instead I say, "I can't believe you're here."

"I live in LA," Odie corrects me. "I can't believe *you're* here."

"Sometimes I can't either."

Behind me, I hear some of the customers whispering. I know I can't just stand here talking to him all night, so I wave him in front of the sign.

"I guess I can let one more in. . . ."

"So generous," Odie says.

He presses his hands deep into his pockets, like he doesn't quite know what to do with them. I smile at him again and climb back into the truck.

The line inches along slowly. I can see him there, in the

back, watching as I ring up each customer. Listening to my awkward small talk, how I try to answer questions or make recommendations based on the dwindling selection. I'm not surprised he saw I was in LA—I didn't try to hide it on Crushed's Instagram feed—but I am surprised he came to see me. We haven't spoken in almost a year.

After his parents gave me that check, I felt so strange about it, but there was nothing I could do. They wouldn't take it back. Odie and I had already stopped talking as much and I didn't want him to think it was permission for him to come back in my life whenever he wanted. I just wanted to move forward for once and not be so caught up in the past.

But the truth was, I never stopped wondering what he was doing. I muted his Instagram page, but I'd still check it every so often. When the news broke that his parents had settled out of court with Brett's family, I was happy for him, celebrating in my own quiet way. I wanted to text him or call . . . but by that time it didn't feel right anymore. I'd seen a picture of a new girl in one of his photos, and I worried he might be dating someone.

The line keeps inching along. He's still there, in the back, still watching me. When the last customers finally leave, instead of standing there and trying to talk through the window, I bring the very last cupcake down to him and close up the back of the truck.

"Hey . . . I wanted to be a paying customer," he says. "It's only right."

"I think you're an investor, technically."

"I'm definitely not."

He immediately takes a bite, mmming and aahing the same way he did in the inn's kitchen a year ago. When he's done, he sits down on the truck's bumper and looks up at me.

"You're in LA," he says.

"I'm sorry I didn't tell you."

I'm not sorry, though—not really. If I'd told him I was moving here it would've become all about him . . . and us. What did it mean? Did he still have feelings for me? Could we make it work? I would've been consulting him about where I got an apartment, about what events to bring the truck to or which places I should hang out at.

I wanted this move to be just for me.

"I saw you were in LA too still and . . ." I start.

"It seemed like a lot of pressure. I get it."

"It's just been a while."

"Too long, Callie."

He looks away, down at some crumpled wrappers on the pavement. Behind us, one of the live bands starts another number. It's slow and mournful. Something about telling everyone it's your song.

"You're here, though," I say. "That must feel good."

"I got into UCLA. I got an academic scholarship, but I took out loans for the rest. I basically didn't give my parents a say."

"Wow," I say.

It's beyond impressive. Odie is actually doing what he said he was going to do. All the time I spent worrying about what his parents thought of me, or how the photo ruined everything . . . it's like he's finally broken free of them. Does it really matter what they think if he's living on his own now? If he's forging his own path?

I haven't looked in a mirror in hours and I'm suddenly self-conscious. This isn't exactly how I imagined we'd run into each other again. When I've played it out I'm always older, more successful, usually wearing some kind of vintage silk dress that hugs me in all the right places. Right now my apron is still on, and I'm sure there are bits of frosting stuck in my hair.

"This is amazing, Callie. You're really doing it."

"Something like that. . . ."

But I'm already smiling.

"I hope you don't mind that I came," he says. "I just saw the *LAist* article, and there was that picture of you, and . . ."

"No, of course I don't mind."

I sit down on the bumper beside him. Our shoulders touch and I feel that electric charge again, the thrill of being close to him. It's true I didn't imagine it like this, but I'm still grateful it's happening. That we're here together.

"You said I would stop, but I didn't," he says.

Loving me, is what he means. I said he'd stop loving me.

I don't need him to explain it. I remember every word of that conversation, and these feelings haven't gone away for me either, even when I wished they would. It would've been easier if I could've just put Odie out of my mind.

This past spring I dated one of guys who works at the beach club. When that ended, I went out a few times with one of the scuba instructors who lives on the island year-round. But with both of them, and every other guy I've met . . . I'm always comparing them to Odie. Even on my best days with other guys, I didn't feel a fraction of what I'd felt for him.

"I didn't either. . . ." I finally admit. "I never stopped."

It's all the confirmation he needs. He grabs my hand and pulls it to his heart. I let my head rest on his shoulder and close my eyes, breathing in that familiar smell. It's been over a year but it doesn't feel like any time has passed. It's like we're still back in that room now, or lying on the beach beside the sea caves.

"Should we get some food?" he asks. "We could try—"

"Pita's actually here," I say. "She's visiting me for a few days."

"Oh . . ."

"No, it's good—it's just . . ." I say, knowing I can't just ditch my best friend because Odie came back. I owe her more than that. "This weekend is supposed to be about us."

His expression shifts, and he seems disappointed. "Should I go, then?"

"I'll just . . . I'll see you Monday. And probably every day after that. Does that work?"

He laughs, relieved. "Wherever you want, I'll be there."

Odie stands and wraps me in a tight hug, and I feel like things make sense again. Like everything is working out the way it's supposed to. Odie is at UCLA. I'm making about a gazillion desserts a week, and already thinking about buying another food truck, or at least hiring someone to help me.

And we're together now.

I give him a kiss on the cheek before I say goodbye.